"Damn, I wish you weren't married."

Spencer had been teasing, but the minute he said the words, he wanted to swallow them. Jane's hand flew to her mouth in surprise. She looked at the ring on her hand as if she'd never seen it before.

He grabbed his suit jacket off the back of the chair and slipped it on. "I should be going. Thanks for dinner, Jane. And don't work any more tonight."

"But the sales meeting's tomorrow. I wanted to have the new proposal finished."

"Relax. Whenever you finish it, drop it by my receptionist's desk. You don't even have to see the big bad wolf."

"I don't..."

"Avoid me? You do. And your instincts are right on."

"They are?" She sounded as though she wanted him to prove her wrong.

"Oh, yes." Unable to stop himself, he moved closer. Reaching out, he gently ran a finger down her arm. "You know what I'd do right now if you weren't a married woman, don't you?"

Dear Reader,

I know a lot of people who've met their partners through work. It makes sense. You spend a lot of time with your co-workers and love can sometimes result. Or not. I once knew a woman who was so tired of being hit on at her workplace that she bought herself a wedding ring, stuck it on her finger and told everyone she was married.

I thought this idea could be a fun one to explore in a romance. And it was.

Jane Stanford, my heroine, is both a feminist and a romantic. When she starts falling for her boss, those two sides of her nature go to war. And as for the hero, Spencer Tate, he respects women and marriage vows but he soon realizes there is something very strange about Jane's husband....

The course of true love never does run smooth, but the ride can be a lot of fun. I enjoyed getting to know Jane and Spencer. I hope you will, too. As always, I love to hear from readers. You can find me on the Web at http://www.nancywarren.net or write to me at: Nancy Warren, P.O. Box 37035, North Vancouver, B.C. Canada V7N 4M0.

Happy reading,

Nancy Warren

Books by Nancy Warren

FRINGE BENEFITS
Nancy Warren

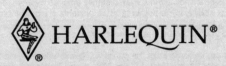

HARLEQUIN®

TORONTO • NEW YORK • LONDON
AMSTERDAM • PARIS • SYDNEY • HAMBURG
STOCKHOLM • ATHENS • TOKYO • MILAN • MADRID
PRAGUE • WARSAW • BUDAPEST • AUCKLAND

For Lois and Roy Reynolds.

Thanks for all your support and encouragement,
and for sharing your son with me.

And, as always, for Rick.

ISBN 0-373-69143-2

FRINGE BENEFITS

Copyright © 2003 by by Nancy Warren.

This edition published by arrangement with Harlequin Books S.A.

Visit us at www.eHarlequin.com

Printed in U.S.A.

1

JANE STANFORD got married on Friday. She celebrated by taking her best friend Alicia Margolin out to dinner.

Jane watched in amusement as Alicia drooled over the chalkboard specials. They were at the chicest new seafood restaurant in Vancouver's trendy Yaletown.

"I'm starving. I heard this place is fabulous, but Chuck's too cheap to bring me here," Alicia complained, gazing at the black ceiling hung with industrial steel lighting, the leather-covered walls, terracotta-tile floor and polished cedar tables as though committing them to memory. "Wait till I tell him you treated me to dinner here. Are we celebrating that you don't have to work with me anymore?"

Jane smiled mischievously. "We're celebrating all right, but not that."

Alicia's eyes widened. "You got a new job?"

"Not yet." Jane's stomach dropped and her appetite deserted her. She wasn't here to dwell on the past, she reminded herself. She was taking steps to ensure a successful future.

As though she were a magician, Jane flourished her left hand in front of Alicia's face. On the fourth finger glowed a thick gold band inset with diamonds.

Alicia gaped.

"I got married."

"Whaaat?" The restaurant's noise level dropped as curious heads turned to stare at the shrieking Alicia. Lowering her voice to a frantic whisper, she demanded, "When? Why didn't I know anything about it? How could you not invite me? I'm your best friend? And..." Alicia stopped for a breath and then a puzzled expression spread across her face. "Who the hell is he?"

Jane decided to answer the last, and most important question, first. "He's the best husband in the world." She leaned back, swirling wine in her glass as she contemplated the utter perfection of her spouse. "He never leaves the toilet seat up or drops dirty clothes around the house. He doesn't drink, gamble or smoke." She glanced at Alicia and couldn't help adding, "He encourages me to buy anything I want."

"Come on." Alicia snorted. "No such guy exists."

Jane smiled in pure bliss. "Exactly."

"What do you mean, 'exactly'?"

"I got the idea after I got fired," Jane began.

"Look, honey, you got a rotten break. Your self-esteem's taken a beating. But if you married that guy Owen who spends all his time with fish guts—"

"He's a marine biologist and no, I didn't marry Owen. I didn't really marry anyone. I'm pretending to be married."

Alicia waited in barely suppressed impatience as the waiter arrived with their food. She hardly glanced at her plate and waved away an offer of fresh-ground pepper. When he'd moved on she said, "Have you lost your mind?"

"No, I haven't." Jane felt the bitterness rise in her

throat. "I'm sick of being hassled by jerks like Phil Johnson just because I'm single and travel a lot on business. Men like Phil consider getting me into bed as a personal challenge. I've tried assertiveness training, self-defense for women—which is how Johnson got the black eye—I dress like a nun—"

"It's your looks," Alicia interrupted. "You could *be* a nun and it wouldn't stop guys from falling for you." She bit into a prawn. "If I wasn't your best friend, I'd hate you."

"Married women don't get hassled all the time. You don't."

"On second thought, I do hate you."

"Having a husband means I don't have to make up a bunch of lame excuses when I'm not interested in a guy. This way, I get all the benefits of being married without having a man underfoot all the time. So, what do you think?"

"I think it's the dumbest idea I've ever heard," Alicia said bluntly. "What about the wedding night?"

Jane raised her chin. "This is it."

Alicia's lips curved in a smug grin. "There's one benefit to being married you seem to forget."

"If you mean sex, I can have as much fun watching an old movie on TV, without having to deal with snoring in my ear afterward."

Her friend's black curls danced as she shook her head. "What happens when you meet a man who makes your toes curl?"

"I'll go to a podiatrist and get them fixed."

"It's obvious you've never been in love." Alicia's

hand flitted across the table to touch Jane's. "Don't do it. There are still good men out there."

Why did married people always act as if she was deficient? Of course, there were good men out there. There were also faithful basset hounds and talking parrots. She didn't want any of them.

"I don't want love. I want a career. I want to be taken seriously and allowed to go as far as I can. Between mother trying to marry me to the 'right people' and all the men I've met in my life, I figure if I was going to fall in love, I would have by now."

"Can't you see? You're overreacting to getting fired. I still think you should sue for sexual harassment."

Jane sighed, pushing away her half-eaten salmon. "I already talked to my lawyer. Punching Johnson wasn't too smart. It's called battery or assault or something. If I sue for sexual harassment, he'll claim I beat him up. You know what a weasel he is. And besides, nobody saw him grab my breast in the elevator, but lots of people saw me hit him."

Alicia chuckled. "He came flying out of that elevator as if somebody'd shot him, blood pouring out his nose. I'll treasure that memory forever." She sobered quickly. "It's not fair you got fired."

"No. It isn't." She still felt sick at how easily that pervert had sabotaged her career, and at how ready their boss—their male boss—had been to ignore her side of the story. It wasn't fair. She'd worked so hard, played by the rules—but they were men's rules. Well, from now on she had a man on her team. Her fictitious husband. "As far as I'm concerned, the playing field just got more even."

Alicia stared at her as though seriously considering her idea for the first time this evening. Jane felt a stirring of hope that her best friend would support her, until she saw her shake her head. "It might work if you weren't the worst liar on the planet."

"I never lie."

"Exactly. For a salesperson, you are so honest it's embarrassing." Her friend chuckled. "Remember when you were supposed to keep my surprise birthday party a secret?"

"I never told a soul."

The chuckle turned into a snort. "Hon, your face broadcast the news every time you tried to tell me a whopper. Believe me, you are not cut out to live a double life."

"But this isn't like lying." Well, she supposed it was in a way. "It's only a little white lie. No one can possibly get hurt because of it. And the benefits far outweigh the obstacles." She thought about how much her career had suffered because she was single and was more determined than ever to go through with her plan.

"No. My mind's made up." She tapped her new ring against the wineglass and raised it in a mock toast. "To Mr. Stanford."

Alicia didn't raise her glass. A small frown marred her usually smiling face. "Johnson's taking credit for the Marsden Holt deal."

The wineglass came back down. "I know. I worked my butt off for that deal. They'd just promised to buy the new inventory system when Johnson started pawing me in the elevator to 'celebrate.'"

"Ooh, he makes me so mad. I can't believe he's getting away with it." Alicia stabbed another prawn so viciously it split in half.

"Maybe he won't."

Her friend paused, the half prawn nearly to her mouth, and glanced up hopefully.

"I have an interview at Datatracker on Monday."

"Datatracker? I read a feature about the president, Spencer Tate. He's one of those dot-com guys who managed to keep some of his millions and stay afloat. And honey, he's cu-ute. Bill Gates's brain and Harrison Ford's looks. Harrison Ford when he was a lot younger, that is."

"Really? *Star Wars* young?" Jane asked, intrigued in spite of herself.

Alicia pondered. "More like *Working Girl* young. I'm telling you, leave the ring at home."

"He's probably married. Anyway, the only thing worse than sleeping with a married man would be sleeping with my boss. Weren't you listening? I'm serious about my work. Sleeping with the boss is career suicide."

"Couldn't you—"

"All I want him checking out is my résumé. In the last couple of years, Datatracker has become our—I mean your—sharpest competitor." She tapped her neatly manicured nails on the tabletop. "I don't think I'm a vengeful woman, but I'll enjoy being Johnson's competition."

"Well I hope you steal all our clients," her loyal friend exclaimed. "Then come headhunting for me."

"I haven't even had an interview yet, although I've

crossed paths with a few Datatracker sales people."
She shrugged. "I want to get a feel for the place, see if I
fit in. I can't afford to make another mistake."

Alicia nodded. "Check out their sexual-harassment
policy."

As they were leaving, a guy in a business suit
reached in front of Jane to open the restaurant door for
them. She turned back with a smile of thanks. There
were two men, and they had the out-of-town look to
them. She knew it well.

The one holding the door blinked at her. His companion sidled closer. "Hey, how would you ladies like
to—"

Jane stuck her left hand in the air letting the light
catch the cold gleam of diamonds. "We're married,"
she said curtly.

"Sure." The spokesman backed off, bumping into
his friend. "Can't blame a guy for trying."

As they walked out of the restaurant, Jane whispered to Alicia, "Still think it's the dumbest idea
you've ever heard?"

Jane didn't. In fact, she thought the imaginary Mr.
Stanford was one of her more brilliant ideas. He was
her ticket to the future.

JANE TWISTED the unfamiliar ring, hoping it would
bring her luck as well as insurance against creeps.
When the young Asian woman called out, "Ms. Stanford?" she rose and got ready to do what she did best:
sell something. This time, it was herself.

"Please come this way."

The woman led her through a maze of cubicles

where intense-looking computer types pecked at keyboards or drew intricate diagrams on white boards. Most of them looked like extras from one of those nerd movies.

A short hallway later she was ushered into the president's office.

She blinked in surprise at the chaotic atmosphere of Spencer Tate's office. She was equally surprised by the tall, dark-haired man who rose from behind the cluttered desk. He was younger than she had expected—mid-thirties she guessed as he stepped forward and extended his hand, the handshake warm and firm.

"Spencer," he introduced himself informally. She was surprised at what a mellow voice he had for a man who was known to be a hard-driving workaholic.

Then he smiled and surprised her even more. *Boyish charm* Jane thought. He oozed it. He had a look that made you want to forgive him anything, 'cause he was just so darn cute, he probably didn't mean it. She bet he got away with murder.

Jane returned the smile. "Jane Stanford."

Spencer Tate gestured to a gray leather armchair and, instead of moving back behind his desk, picked up a file folder and sat in the matching armchair beside Jane. So he wasn't into intimidation by furniture, Jane mused. Good.

While he settled himself and flicked through the folder, Jane studied him surreptitiously. The first thing she noticed was that he needed a haircut. His brown hair trailed over his ears and the back of his collar. His tie needed straightening. His shirt was rumpled and it was coming untucked from his pants.

His body was in great shape, though. Which was more than she could say for his desk, a definite fire hazard with papers littered everywhere and three computers humming at once. The huge whiteboard behind his desk was covered with incomprehensible scribbles that would have done Einstein proud. He looked a lot more like one of the eggheads in Research and Development, where Jane knew he'd started his career, than the CEO of one of the fastest-growing high-tech firms in the country.

While they hadn't exactly thrived during the dot-com bust, Datatracker hadn't gone under either. She wondered how much the man in front of her was responsible for that small miracle.

He cleared his throat before raising assessing brown eyes to hers. They weren't the eyes of a boy or an eccentric scientist. They were all grown up, giving Jane the impression that the naughty-boy exterior hid a steel-trap mind.

"I'm surprised you left Graham's. It's a good firm."

Jane had expected this question. She and her lawyer had agreed that her reputation was the most important thing to salvage from her last job. Each party had signed an agreement not to disparage the other. She had a glowing letter of recommendation from Charles Graham. In return, she had promised to reveal nothing derogatory about her former employer.

"It's a very good firm." Jane parroted her rehearsed answer. "I just felt I needed a change."

He stared at her keenly for a moment, but she wasn't going to be rattled into saying more than she'd planned. He nodded. His gaze dropped back to the pages in front of him. "You have an impressive sales record."

"Thank you. I like to work hard."

He grinned at that, and Jane felt his charm waft over her like a warm tropical breeze. "You'll fit in here, then. I'm a workaholic. My assistant, Yumi, complains all the time but works harder than I do. Despite the workload, we're a pretty loose outfit and work on a principle of trust. But as I said, there's a lot of stress, deadlines, late nights at the office.... Can you work in that kind of environment?"

Jane was puzzled until she realized he was looking at her shiny new wedding ring. "I enjoy what I do, Mr. Tate. I take my job very seriously."

"It's Spencer," he said. "Look, your personal life is none of my business. I just want to be clear about things. To be blunt, this company has already wrecked my own marriage. I don't want to see anybody else's go down because of it."

Jane leaned forward. "Believe me, this job won't wreck my marriage."

"I assume you know there will be a lot of traveling." He glanced up, and she noticed how rich a brown his eyes were—and they twinkled. Espresso on a sunny day, she thought dreamily.

In the two years she'd been in this industry she'd heard a lot about Spencer Tate. People used epithets such as *wily, brilliant, driven,* and *creative* to describe him. They'd forgotten to mention the one that struck her now—the guy was *gorgeous*.

He was still watching her, eyebrows raised, obviously waiting for a response. She played back the last part of the conversation in her head, then nodded. "Yes, I'm accustomed to traveling often."

"I believe you have some languages?"

She nodded again. "French and German, enough Italian to get by. I did some schooling in Switzerland."

"Business college?" He appeared interested.

Jane felt the heat of embarrassment, tried to keep it from her cheeks. "Finishing school."

"Didn't you like being finished?"

No, she hadn't. She'd wanted to go to college, but her parents had wanted her to meet the right man, join the right clubs, have the right children. In fact, they still did. But this was a job interview, not a therapist's couch, so she shrugged and said, "Finishing school is a bit old-fashioned, but I loved Europe and I have a knack for languages."

He leaned back in his chair and crossed an ankle over the opposite knee. "So, why do you want to work here?"

"I've been selling against you for two years now, so I know a lot about your company. You're aggressive, well-respected and growing fast. If I can be frank...?" She waited for his nod before going on with her sales pitch. "Your biggest weakness is your sales team. I see an excellent opportunity here for both of us."

His gaze never left her face as she spoke, and he didn't answer her directly. "My company's been losing accounts we deserve to win. Mostly to Graham's." He leaned back in the leather chair and stretched his long legs. "I'm surprised you could sell Graham's system when you must know our product is better."

"Graham's is a bigger firm," she said. "With a steady history of reliable products."

"Our leading edge system is cheaper to install and breaks down less frequently," he countered, as though he were boasting about a favorite child.

"Leading edge or bleeding edge?" Jane stopped herself when she realized he'd manipulated her into giving a sales pitch for her old company.

"So that's how you've been winning my accounts," he said, assessing her boldly now. "Could you sell our system as convincingly as you sell Graham's?"

She answered honestly. "If I believe in it. And from what I've seen, that shouldn't be a problem."

He gazed at her as though he couldn't make up his mind about something. His gaze strayed to her wedding ring a couple of times. What was that all about? Did the man not know it was not only politically incorrect but illegal to make hiring decisions based on a person's marital status? She felt like screaming. Single or married, she just couldn't seem to win.

"I think our base salary is a little lower than your previous firm's, but the commission is more generous. If you're as good as I think you are, you should end up making more money with us."

She hesitated, unconsciously turning the unfamiliar ring round on her finger. "Money doesn't motivate me as much as other factors." She took a breath. Might as well get to the point. "I'm a bit of an overachiever. I love selling, but my eventual plan is to move up into an executive capacity. How would you feel about that?"

She watched him carefully for signs of chauvinism or hostility, but all she saw was understanding. Talk about overachievers. She and Spencer Tate were two of a kind.

"This company is growing fast, and will keep growing. Your career will grow with it. If things work out, you could easily move to an executive position. Hell, I don't know how long I'll be here. Maybe you'll end up as the CEO."

Her heart was beating a little faster. "You mean that?"

"Absolutely."

She was suddenly glad she'd lost her old job. She already felt as though she'd fit in here.

"I'll get Yumi to give you a tour of the place. Talk to anyone you like. Ask them anything."

He talked about Datatracker then. Jane could see his pride in the company and its people. He asked a few more questions and she told him more about her schooling and career to this point. It was an odd job interview. Jane had the sensation that she was chatting with someone she'd known for a long time. She felt at ease with him. Her instincts told her she could trust him. And, after the last career fiasco, trust was important. They talked for almost an hour, but it seemed as if she'd only been in his office a few minutes.

"It was nice to meet you. I'll be in touch," he said.

"Nice to meet you, too," Jane replied and rose to

leave. He stood and she extended her hand. His hand closed over hers, firm and warm. To her shock and horror, a sizzle of male/female awareness passed between them. She pulled her hand back immediately.

He'd as good as told her he was single. Her hormones had told her he was sexually attractive.

Thank goodness she had her "husband" to keep either of them from getting any ideas that weren't strictly business.

2

GOOD THING she's married, Spencer thought, watching Jane Stanford's retreating form. Otherwise she could be very distracting. He noticed again the way her navy suit couldn't disguise her curvaceous woman's body.

Her golden-blond hair was squished into a coil at the back of her neck, but the few strands that had escaped curled provocatively. And she didn't need makeup to emphasize blue eyes that had a hint of purple in their depths, or the full-lipped mouth.

She reminded him of somebody, and in a moment he realized it was Miss September who'd been peeping down from the cement wall of the auto mechanic's garage when he'd had his car serviced the day before. She had the same full lips that seemed to be begging for kisses, similarly luminous big blue eyes. And the boxy jacket couldn't hide the full breasts that could have graced any centerfold. He shook his head to clear it of a sudden vision of Jane in nothing but the jacket—coyly unbuttoned and hanging open to reveal...

That sexy mouth had talked a lot of clients into buying expensive computer systems, and that's what he was supposed to be thinking about. She might look as desirable in her business suit as Miss September in lingerie, but she was off-limits.

He rustled the pages inside the file folder in front of

him while he marshaled his impressions. She came
across as intelligent, classy. She had a nice personality
without being pushy. He felt she was a person he could
like and work with easily. But one thing bothered him.
She didn't seem the type to leave a solid outfit on a
whim. Not when she'd been making a good name for
herself.

He picked up the phone and dialed the direct number of an old friend who happened to work for Graham's.

The information he was looking for cost him a couple of drinks at a trendy martini bar. By the time he had
the whole story, he wanted to blacken the SOB's other
eye. Spencer didn't like men who hassled women on
the job. And guys who made up to married women
made him sick.

The news that Jane had decked some clown who
didn't respect office protocol or marriage vows didn't
bother him in the least. In fact, he respected her for it.
More than he respected her former CEO, who, in Spencer's opinion, had fired the wrong person.

He'd discovered another piece of information over
the second martini. Turned out the deal hadn't been
sealed with a very lucrative client that Jane had
brought in.

He thought about that while he ate cold pizza at
home, watching a hockey game. He'd give up one or
two less important body parts if he could nab a client
like Marsden Holt.

He wondered if Ms. Stanford would be interested in
a spot of revenge?

He was still thinking about it the next morning at work when he dialed her home number.

"Hello?" Her voice was pleasant on the phone he noted. A real asset for a sales person.

"Good morning, Jane. Spence Tate calling."

"Hi! I didn't expect to hear from you so soon."

"So what do you think of our operation?"

"I'm impressed. I think your system is better than Graham's, and it's certainly a better value for the customer. Datatracker's atmosphere is relaxed but hardworking. Your staff seem happy."

She might be trying to butter him up to get the job, but Spence didn't think so. She sounded sincere and he felt puffed up by the compliment. "I'm calling to offer you the job."

"Wonderful. I accept."

He didn't realize how worried he'd been that she might turn him down. Her acceptance sent a jab of excitement to his belly. "Great, when can you start?"

"How about Monday?"

"How about tomorrow? I uh, have a project I want to get started on right away."

Her laugh was low and musical. "You did warn me you were a slave driver, didn't you?"

"No." He smiled into the receiver. "You assured me you're a workaholic."

"Sounds like we were both right. I'll see you tomorrow."

Spencer was still smiling when he got on the intercom to Yumi. "Bring in the file on Marsden Holt, will you?"

"You been chasing parked cars again?" Yumi asked sweetly as she dropped the dog-eared file on his desk.

"We are going to get Marsden Holt, Yumi. Jane came close to bagging the account at her last job—but the contract hasn't officially been awarded yet." He leaned back and crossed his arms behind his head. "She made the sale once. Maybe she can make it again with our superior product."

He brought his hands down and banged out a drum roll on the desktop. "It'll be like stealing candy from a baby."

JANE SIPPED cool white wine thankfully. Her feet had swollen on the plane and pinched inside her pumps. Her hair was crisp with static electricity and her skin felt dry. What she really wanted was a long soak in a hot bath slick with scented oils and maybe a relaxing candle or two flickering on the ledge. But, with one more flight to go before reaching home, she was settling for a drink with Spencer in an airport lounge at O'Hare.

She had never experienced a more hectic three weeks. She was learning the Datatracker system, memorizing the sales record of her new company, visiting existing customers to see the system at work. And wooing Marsden Holt.

Again.

After her phone call, Marsden Holt had agreed to take a second look at Datatracker. She supposed that they were doing it as a favor to her and they weren't really serious, but she loved a tough sell the way some people love a complicated puzzle. She wanted this account just as much as her new boss did, and for entirely personal reasons.

Spence had seemed ready to talk her into going after them, but in fact she'd been delighted to have the opportunity. This time, her revenge on Johnson would be bloodless but far more satisfying.

She knew from the other salespeople how rare it was for Spence to go along on a sales trip. She'd thought he'd made the trip to Marsden Holt's head office in Detroit partly because she was so new. But now she realized there was more to it than that. For some reason he really wanted this one. He'd let her take the meeting, answering only the questions that were directed at him. But the presence of the CEO had sent a clear message to the client.

He drank deeply from a frosted beer mug. "Mmm. Well, I thought the presentation went pretty well. What did you think? You know them better than I do."

Jane wiggled her toes, wondering if she'd ever get her circulation back. "I think it went well." In fact, there was a niggle of excitement under her breastbone.

Spencer nodded, rotating his shoulders.

It was the first sign of tension she'd seen in him. She'd hardly recognized him when he'd shown up for the presentation in a perfectly pressed gray suit, burgundy silk tie, crisp white shirt and shiny black shoes. He'd even had his hair cut.

Now that he was relaxing, he was starting to rumple. His suit jacket hung lopsided on his chair back and his hair looked as if he'd been running his hands through it. He loosened the knot on his tie, pulling the silk askew, and undid his top shirt button.

She watched the movement of muscle beneath the shirt and for a moment imagined his naked torso. It would be fit and strong. She remembered seeing a tennis racquet in his office. Maybe that was how he stayed in shape. The images her mind was projecting caused a tingle of excitement deep inside, swiftly followed by horror. What was she thinking?

She glanced up to find his eyes on hers, a disturbing light in them. She glanced away and took refuge in another sip of wine.

"So," he said gruffly. "Tell me about your husband."

Jane swallowed too quickly and the wine went down the wrong way making her gasp and splutter. "My wh-what?"

"Your husband. The guy you married?"

"Oh, him." She sat back, wiped her eyes on a napkin. "Well, let's see." She should have thought this through, she realized, invented some fantasy husband to go along with the ring. Added some color to her little white lie. Now her mind was completely blank.

Seconds ticked by. She was a practical woman. Flights of fancy were not her forté, especially when she was footsore and exhausted. Her husband was an abstract concept, a personal gatekeeper and no more. She'd never bothered to give him any more substance than as the fictional purchaser of The Ring.

Now that she was being asked to produce more evidence of his existence she felt panic-stricken. Her gaze searched the bar for a guy she could use as a model for her life partner.

"Well, he's..." But the men lounging in wooden chairs or slouched at the bar looked like tired business-

men; baggy-eyed, slack-jawed and a lot more interested in the golf game flickering on the overhead TV
than they were in being her husband.

"He's um..." She cleared her throat and glanced at
the TV screen while a trickle of sweat slid between her
breasts, hoping against hope that maybe a golf pro
could inspire her. But just as she began to study the little figures in their pastel sweaters and golf hats the
screen flashed to a commercial.

She was just about to start babbling anything at all
when she saw him, grinning down at her like the answer to her dreams.

Tom Cruise, in an ad for his new movie.

Her lips tilted. He was the perfect fantasy husband—
and he'd been her first love after all.

Jane sighed and silently thanked Hollywood for giving her the perfect mate.

"He's very handsome," she gushed. "Black hair,
blue eyes, great smile." She turned her attention back
to Spencer and realized with a shock that looking at
him gave her a similar thrill to the one Tom had ignited
in her teenage heart.

"Known him long?"

"I've had a crush on him since high school." Jane
had a mental picture of him singing in his underpants
in *Risky Business*. "Oh, yes." She sighed dreamily.
"Quite a crush."

He nodded, appearing truly interested. "You go
back a long way, then."

"First guy I ever kissed." And kissed and kissed and
kissed, until she'd made soggy pulp of a glossy magazine pin-up she'd hung in her room.

"What's he like?" Spence's voice was a little sharp and brought Jane back with a bump from the biggest crush she'd ever had.

"Like?" She shrugged. "He's handsome." As if that explained it all.

"Does he have any hobbies?"

She heard amusement in his tone. She must sound like a drooling idiot. Which was just as well. The more people who thought she was madly in love with her new husband, the safer she would be.

"Oh...um...well...he likes fighter planes." And she'd wanted to trade places with Kelly McGillis when she'd watched *Top Gun* four or five hundred times. "And, race cars, and um...let's see. Vampires!" Ooh, those long teeth when he'd played Lestat had made her shiver.

"Vampires?" Spence cocked an amused eyebrow. "It doesn't sound as though you two have a lot in common."

"Well, sure we do. We both like to travel, for instance."

"Oh, where to?"

"Oh, far and away... I mean Ireland. That's where his family is from, originally. And um, Europe." Well, he'd saved the channel tunnel between England and France single-handedly in *Mission Impossible*. He must have gone there.

"How did you two meet?"

That was easy. "At the movies."

"Is he in sales, too?"

Jane's throat tightened. She'd thought a shiny gold ring on her left hand would do the whole job. It hadn't occurred to her to run a complete profile on her pretend husband.

For the first time, she had an inkling of what Alicia had meant when she called the fake husband idea the stupidest thing she'd ever heard. For a woman who detested untruths, she was spilling lies like water from a gushing faucet. And to Spencer, of all people. If she'd met him before the job interview...

No. She had to stop thinking that way. Business and pleasure didn't mix—she'd believed that even before Phil Johnson let his hands roam in the elevator.

Her boss was the most attractive, interesting man she'd met in a long time. But he was still her boss. She hadn't come this far to end up as a woman who slept with the CEO. Sexy he might be, with his espresso eyes, unruly hair and great body, but he was definitely off-limits.

With an effort, she brought her mind back to Tom Cruise.

"No, he's in the...um...entertainment business."

Her armpits felt uncomfortably warm. She didn't think she could keep this up much longer. Thankfully, she heard a garbled voice coming out of a nearby speaker. She couldn't make out the words and didn't care. She recognized a lifeline when it was tossed her way. "I think that's our flight they're calling." She jumped up and grabbed her briefcase.

"We've still got a few minutes." Spence rose reluctantly, eyeing the last third of his beer.

"I'm anxious to get home, that's all."

Her boss picked up his beer glass and raised it in her direction with a crooked grin. "To newlyweds," he said. But something in his eyes caused her heart to jump.

The business of boarding their last flight and getting seated kept them from any more personal conversation, and Jane was determined to keep it that way. The minute they sat she took refuge in the pages of *Computing World* magazine. Doggedly she read about the latest advances in chip design and new products on the market, anything to avoid conversing with the man beside her about her "husband."

Spencer perused the *Wall Street Journal*. It was hot and airless on the plane and soon Jane removed her suit jacket. Without raising his head from the paper, Spence held the neck for her while she wriggled out of the scratchy wool sleeves.

Minutes later he took off his own jacket.

Their arms barely touched on the shared armrest, but through the silk of her blouse Jane felt the warmth radiating from his skin through his cotton shirt. The flow of heat back and forth was like a quiet conversation.

Neither of them moved, both seemingly absorbed in their reading material. But it was a long time before either turned a page.

Spence tried to concentrate on the business news, but his thoughts were tormented by the woman beside him. She was wearing a silk blouse under that tailored jacket as opposed to the masculine shirt he'd expected—and he'd definitely caught the shadow of a lacy camisole. It showed a feminine softness so unexpected that Spencer experienced an erotic charge just thinking about all that womanly splendor rigidly covered up.

In an age when nudity was something he saw all the time on TV and the movies, even at the beach, he felt like an old-fashioned gent who'd just caught sight of a lady's ankle.

He rustled the page as he turned it with determination. He'd been diligently reading for pages without making sense of a single article. His cheek itched. He rubbed it impatiently.

She's married, she's married, she's married, he chanted inside his head while he felt the delicious warmth of her skin burning through his shirt. She didn't wear perfume, but her own soft and womanly scent teased his senses. He rustled his way to the stock listings. "Hmm. High-tech stocks are up today, but lumber companies are down. I wonder why?"

Her arm brushed against his as she turned her body toward him. "Did you miss the front page?" She leaned over him, closing the paper. She pointed to the blaring headline "Consumer Survey Predicts Computer Sales Will Rise, Housing Starts Fall." He'd read the entire article and hadn't remembered a word. He glanced sheepishly at Jane who grinned back.

Up close he could see indigo flecks in the irises of her blue eyes. The odd wisp of cornsilk teased her cheeks where it had escaped from the coil at the back of her neck. Her skin was flawless, smooth and golden and he wondered if it felt as soft as it looked.

He could feel his eyes sending out messages they had no business sending—messages that communicated how much he wanted to kiss those slightly parted lips, how much he wanted to peel away the silk, and touch and taste the skin it covered. He wanted...things he had no right to want of a married woman. He jerked his head away from temptation and back to the business pages.

"Thanks," he muttered.

"You're welcome." Was it his imagination or had that calm voice taken on a decidedly husky note?

3

SPENCER SCRUNCHED the paper cup from his first take-out coffee of the day. He'd lain awake thinking about Jane in a totally unprofessional way last night.

He had to admit to himself that he had the biggest crush he'd experienced since college. "But she's married, damn it," he muttered, tossing the mutilated paper coffee cup in the garbage can. It hit the rim with a hollow ping before falling in.

He walked to the window and leaned on the sill, watching the sun tint the top of Grouse Mountain. He'd figured since he couldn't sleep, he might as well come in early and get some work done, but so far he'd only managed to turn on a computer, which hummed quietly on his desk.

Adultery was a dirty word. The ugliest word he knew. He rolled it around on his tongue a few times, reliving in his gut how he felt when he found out about Karen. What a prize fool he'd been, working his brains out to make a better home for his wife and the family they'd planned. She'd thanked him by having an affair, then leaving him.

He turned from the window in disgust. Well, he had principles, and he believed Jane did, too. Even if their attraction was mutual—and based on the way she'd raved about the hubster, that didn't seem likely—there was no way they'd do to Jane's husband what Karen had done to him.

Jane's husband. He'd been amazed at how girlish and excited she'd sounded when describing him. In spite of her obvious infatuation, he couldn't form much of a mental picture of the man. Based on what she had told him, he had a hazy image of a handsome dark-haired man with a lot of odd interests.

It wasn't enough.

Hell, if he wanted a flesh-and-blood reminder, he should meet the guy, get to know him.

He'd finally met the boyfriend of his ex-wife, Karen—after they'd got married. He'd planned to hate him, but Jim turned out to be okay. Surely if he got to know Jane's husband, he wouldn't feel tempted to steal the man's wife.

He realized that that was the smart thing to do, and the sooner the better. He had just the opportunity in mind.

He was elbow-deep in paperwork, his stomach considerably calmed, when Jane walked by his open door.

"Jane," he called out. "Can I see you for a minute?"

She walked in and all his nighttime fantasies came roaring back. He wanted to take the pins out of her hair, slowly. He wanted to unbutton her suit jacket, one brass button at a time. He wanted—

"Did I spill something on myself?" she asked, following his stare.

"No, no. I was just thinking, I have a suit in a similar fabric."

Her brows rose. "Navy pinstripes are very popular

this season," she said. "Is that what you wanted to see me about?"

He shook his head to clear it. "Sorry. I didn't sleep too well last night." He looked up and she was blushing slightly. Had she read his mind? More likely she hadn't slept much either, burning up the sheets with that dark-haired, multi-talented husband.

Spence cleared his throat, and riffled through the papers on his desk looking for his day planner. "I wanted to talk to you about the company's annual general meeting."

"All right."

"As you know, everyone on the payroll is a shareholder. We combine the meeting with a party. We have a tradition around here. We always let the newest hire pick the date. It's our big chance of the year to dress up and meet one another's spouses."

"Spouses?" The blush had receded; now she looked as white as her blouse.

"Well, spouses for those who have them, dates for those who don't. But you'll bring your husband, of course."

"Oh, well...I'm not sure. He travels a lot." She was fiddling with her briefcase.

"That's why I'm telling you now, so you can talk over your schedule with him. You pick the day, we'll work around it. We're all looking forward to meeting him."

She sat down in the chair across from him as though her legs had buckled. "Look, it's not that simple, Spence."

Hope fought with concern as he looked at her pale

face. "Is everything all right with you two? It's none of my business, but I'm divorced." He gestured in a way he was pretty sure he'd seen Dr. Phil do on TV. "If you need someone to talk to, the door's always open."

"Oh, no. It's nothing like that." She laughed a bit hysterically. "Of course he'll come. I'll just take the calendar home and say, 'Honey, we have a date!'" She nodded sharply. "I'm sure he'll be thrilled to meet you. I'll talk it over with him and let you know tomorrow." Where her face had been pale a minute ago, a hectic flush now suffused her cheeks. She leapt to her feet and dashed out of the door so fast his head spun.

He looked after Jane's retreating back with concern. Maybe she was working too hard?

"ALICIA, what am I going to do?" Jane wailed for the fourth or fifth time that minute. An empty wine bottle sat on the floor between the two women facing each other on Alicia's floral loveseat.

"If only I'd thought faster, I could have said my husband and I don't believe in mixing our professional and personal lives. But I panicked. I actually said that my Tom Cruise look-alike hubby would be delighted to come."

"Couldn't you tell him old Tom suddenly got appendicitis?"

"What if Spence wants to send flowers to the hospital or something?"

"What about a dying relative? Out of town?"

Jane rolled her eyes. "Puh-lease!"

"Maybe you could write to Tom Cruise and explain the situation. I'm sure he'd be happy to pretend to be your husband for one night. That's his job, isn't it, pretending to be other people?"

"Alicia, you're brilliant!" Jane beamed at her, sipping from her glass only to find it was empty. Again.

Her friend sent her a worried glance. "Honey, it was a joke."

Jane shook her head violently. "Not that Tom, another Tom." Alicia looked suspiciously at her, then at the empty wine bottle.

"I mean, I'll hire an actor to play my husband for one evening. How hard can that be?"

"One who looks like Tom Cruise?" Alicia rolled her eyes. "I don't know why you had to marry Tom Cruise. You could have picked just some average guy, but oh, no, you have to pick a movie star."

"But he's my husband, Alicia," Jane protested, stung. "I wanted Spence to know I've got good taste in men. Anyway, you don't have to be so literal. I just sort of described my husband as handsome, with blue eyes, black hair and a great smile."

The front door opened and shut. "Hi, honey, I'm home." From down the hall came the voice of Chuck, Alicia's husband.

"We're in here."

Behind the thick lenses of his eyeglasses, Chuck's blue eyes widened as he stared at the two women sprawled on the couch.

Alicia pulled him down for a fond kiss, ruffling his thinning black hair. "I'd offer you a drink, but we finished the bottle. How 'bout opening another one?"

Clucking like a mother hen, Chuck disappeared with the empty bottle into the kitchen, returning with a newly opened full bottle. He filled their glasses and poured himself one.

He sat down and loosened his tie. "So, how are you Jane?" He asked. "How's the new job?"

"Never mind the small talk, Chuck." Alicia spoke before Jane could answer. "Jane's in trouble. She has to find a husband who looks like Tom Cruise in the next four weeks."

"I'll keep my eyes open," Chuck said placidly.

"He doesn't have to look exactly like Tom Cruise. He just has to have black hair and blue eyes, that's all," Jane objected.

"Oh, I see," Chuck said, in the voice of one who has ceased to be surprised by his wife and her friends.

After a few minutes, Chuck leaned closer to Alicia. "How much has Jane had to drink?" he asked softly.

"Why?"

"She keeps staring at me. She's not going to pass out, is she?" He looked at Jane worriedly. "I can't carry any more of your unconscious friends down the elevator and through the lobby and put them into a taxi. It's just plain embarrassing. I've got my reputation to consider, Alicia. In fact, the next time you want to have a New Year's Eve party—"

"Chuck, take off your glasses!" Jane demanded.

"Alicia, I'm going to have to call A.A. Really, it's only six o'clock."

Alicia ignored him, staring at Jane. "You don't mean...you aren't thinking what I think you're thinking...are you?"

Jane nodded enthusiastically, pleased that her friend had caught on so quickly. She gestured to Chuck with the same awe she'd feel in front of the Mona Lisa. "Black Hair! Blue eyes!"

"Doesn't have to look like Tom Cruise," they both shrieked together before looking at the seriously disturbed face of Chuck and back at each other. Then they burst into a duet of chuckles, howls and snickers.

"Take off your glasses, darling," Alicia said, finally wiping her streaming eyes.

"Have you both gone insane?" Chuck demanded.

"Are you sure you don't mind?" Jane asked Alicia.

"Not if you don't," Alicia intoned, which set them off laughing again.

"Oh, no. Absolutely not!" was Chuck's response when, between giggles, Jane and Alicia explained what they wanted him to do. "I am not going to impersonate some fictitious husband who may or may not look like Tom Cruise. What if I bumped into somebody from my accounting firm?"

"You won't, Chuck. The party's in a private room at a French restaurant," Jane said. "I wish you'd think about it. It would save my career," she added in a wheedling tone.

"But I can't pretend to be your husband. I'm already married!"

"Please, honey?" Alicia chimed in.

"I won't go around pretending to be a bigamist, not even for you, dear." His face went from pink to ruddy as Alicia pulled off his glasses, and Jane started moving his hair around trying to make it look thicker. "It's indecent."

"But Chuck, sweetie."

"And that's final, Alicia."

Alicia winked at Jane and pulled her down the hall toward the front door. "Leave him to me," she whispered. "If you don't get any better ideas between now and the party, Chuck will be your date."

"Alicia, I don't want you whispering. I know it's about me and I absolutely refuse to have anything to do with this foolishness."

"Thanks, honey," Jane gave her best friend a quick hug.

"Alicia?" Chuck yelled again from the living room. "Are you listening to me?"

"Of course, if Chuck is your only choice, you might want to rethink the appendicitis," Alicia whispered.

Jane shook her head. "He's perfect."

Alicia rolled her gaze to the ceiling. "I love the man, Jane. But Tom Cruise he's not."

"Don't you see? That's why he's perfect. After Spencer heard me drooling about how handsome Chuck is...and then he sees him...no offense, but he'll have to believe I'm totally in love with the guy."

"Alicia?" Chuck's voice had risen an octave or two. "Don't make me come down there."

Alicia's eyes narrowed. "Wait a minute. What am I missing here? Why do you care whether your boss thinks you're in love with your husband? I thought you just had to produce one?"

"Oh, I just want to make the lie more believable, that's all," Jane said quickly, averting her face before her best friend could read the confusion she felt.

"Jane—"

"Alicia, I am definitely coming down that hallway. I'll count to ten. One, two—"

"You'd better go and start working on him," Jane said, and slipped out the door, thankful to escape Alicia's all-too-penetrating eyes.

She walked the few blocks through the west end to her own apartment, her imagination busily giving Chuck a makeover—something that would make him look a little more like Tom Cruise. The glasses would definitely have to go.

She wondered how he'd feel about a toupee.

4

ONCE THE WINE BUZZ cleared, so did Jane's optimism about Chuck as an ideal date. She was in a trap and couldn't find a way out. Of course, she could do as Alicia had suggested and come down with a convenient flu bug, or inflict on her poor husband any number of catastrophes. But it would only postpone the inevitable.

Besides. It kept happening.

She saw the way Spence looked at her, a warmth in his eyes that wasn't there when he spoke to the rest of the staff. He wasn't the kind of lowlife who made suggestive comments when she walked by, or who groped her when no one else was looking, but it was unprofessional and inappropriate for him to look at her that way. This was the workplace and he was her boss.

It was just as unprofessional and inappropriate for her pulse to flutter when their gazes met. Jane wanted to build a career on her own, without either hindrance or help from a co-worker who found her attractive. If she didn't feel an answering warmth deep inside every time their eyes met, then maybe she would have found an excuse not to produce the husband.

But she was shrewd enough to know that the husband was the only thing that kept the warmth from flaring into passion between her and her boss. She was never going to get where she wanted in life by becoming that offensive cliché—a woman who slept her way to the top.

Chuck was the bucket of cold water to douse the tiny flame that burned between her and one all-too-attractive CEO.

She never knew how Alicia did it, but somehow she brought Chuck around to agreeing to impersonate Jane's husband for one night—though it was clear he was not happy with the task.

Jane wasn't happy about it either, and over the next month as the general meeting and dinner party drew closer she started to lose her nerve. She liked Chuck, but pretending to be in love with him was going to be a stretch. And, as for her stand-in husband, he treated her like a vision of doom whenever she saw him.

She hoped for floods, a small earthquake, anything to keep the party from taking place as scheduled. But Indian summer had set in, bringing flawless warm weather and sunshine. Natural disasters seemed to be happening everywhere in the world but Vancouver, British Columbia.

Jane dithered over her wardrobe. She hated events that mixed business and pleasure. A suit was too businesslike, spaghetti straps too far the other way. She paced back and forth in front of her wardrobe in her bra and panties, thinking. The purpose of tonight's masquerade was to let everyone at the office—and one man in particular—know she had a life outside work. A wildly exciting, happily married life.

She pulled out a purple sueded-silk sheath and nodded. Perfect. It had manicotti, rather than spaghetti, straps that left her arms bare. On the hanger it was demure; on her it was much less so, but she paired it with a hand-dyed raw-silk jacket she'd discovered at a craft fair. She left her hair fluffed loosely about her face so that blond curls teased her cheeks when she moved. The dress brought out the color in her eyes, and she added a little more makeup than usual.

Nerves jumped and popped throughout her system. She sat at her dressing table in front of the mirror and forced herself to relax and visualize a successful evening. Visualization exercises worked for sales presentations, and she'd used them to improve her skiing abilities. They ought to help her manufacture a happy marriage for a single evening.

Deliberately, she pulled up Chuck's image and her confidence immediately wavered. Another deep, slow breath and she tried again. She imagined Chuck on her arm and forced a smile as she checked herself out in the mirror. "See how much fun I'm having being married?" she said aloud.

Chuck was right on time, for which she thanked Alicia's bullying and his own passion for punctuality. He looked so miserable, Jane wanted to give him a hug. "How did she make you do it?"

Chuck sent her a half grin. "If you were married—which I deeply wish you were—you wouldn't have to ask questions like that."

"Right." She touched his shoulder. "We'll leave just as soon as dinner is over, Chuck. I can't tell you how much I appreciate this."

"Let's just get it over with."

His expression might not say, "See how much fun

I'm having being married?" but at least he'd dressed for the part. He wore a gray suit, shiny black shoes, white shirt and a jaunty tie that Alicia must have chosen. His hair was no thicker, but someone, no doubt his real wife, had done their best to give it some style.

"Remember, if anyone asks, you're in the entertainment business," she reminded him as their cab pulled up to the restaurant.

"Entertainment business?" He stared at her as though she'd lost her mind.

"Yes. Alicia promised she'd prep you on your part."

But when she saw Chuck's hunted expression, and the way he kept glancing at the cab driver as though trying to find the courage to tell him to turn around, she understood why Alicia hadn't fully prepped Chuck.

"Never mind," she said as cheerfully as a woman facing certain doom can, "We'll wing it."

When they arrived at the restaurant, Jane stopped him at the door. "Please Chuck, the glasses?"

"Jane, without these glasses I border on legally blind."

"I'll hold your hand and guide you, I promise."

With a mutter of protest he snatched them off his face and carefully put them away in a protective case.

"I can barely see," he whispered urgently as she pulled him into the lighted restaurant, holding tightly to his hand so he couldn't bolt.

The first person she bumped into was Yumi, gorgeous in red and black.

"This is my husband, Taro. He doesn't speak very good English. He's only been here one year."

"Good evening." He bowed to Jane.

"Ohio go sai mus," Jane said, bowing back.

"Ha, you speak better Japanese than Spencer. Hey, Boss," Yumi turned and called over her shoulder, "maybe you should send Jane to Tokyo next time."

Jane looked past Yumi and felt her stomach contract. Spencer in a crisp new business suit was quite a sight. His hair was freshly cut and his shoes were polished. As he walked toward her, she had to drag in a breath. He was looking at her not as a CEO looks at his newest salesperson, but as a man looks at a woman. The atmosphere between them was suddenly charged.

He broke the spell first, "Wow," he said. "You look great when you take your business suit off." He flushed immediately, "I mean in a dress. Oh, hell." He laughed. "You know what I mean."

"You're hurting my hand," Chuck whispered anxiously in Jane's ear. She let go of the vise grip she had on him, and, glad of his presence, made the introductions.

Spencer glanced at Chuck, then at Jane, and once more at Chuck, "This is the guy you were telling me about in the airport?" He appeared stunned. Jane remembered how she'd gushed, and felt a giggle threaten. She'd described a movie star and shown up with a balding, nearsighted accountant.

"We were high-school sweethearts," she cooed, kissing Chuck's cheek. *See how happy I am to be married to Chuck?*

He jumped a mile at her improvised kiss, then tried to make amends. He gazed vaguely around the group of faces. "That's right. High-school sweethearts." He reached out a hand to pat her. He was going for her shoulder, but she was taller than Alicia. He caught her breast and then jumped another mile. She was tempted to do the same. They'd been here less than five minutes and she wanted to bolt.

Spencer had recovered from his stupor and was looking at them oddly. Jane desperately hoped it was confusion and not suspicion she read in his eyes. She put on a bright smile and ruffled Chuck's hair fondly, the way she'd seen Alicia do it. "First love, only love," she cooed to the rapidly reddening Chuck.

An elegant woman arrived to stand beside Spencer. She had long curly red hair that floated over her shoulders. Her cocktail-length black gown showed off a statuesque body. Spencer turned his head and smiled at her affectionately.

Jane tried not to gape. She could have saved herself the trouble of dragging poor Chuck to this event. Clearly, Spencer had a woman. How stupid of her to have let a couple of warm glances get to her like this. Though, if she were honest with herself, she'd have to admit it wasn't Spence's gazes that bothered her so much as her own unusually warm response.

"Jane and Chuck, I'd like you to meet Chelsea."

Jane had spent so much time obsessing about Spence's reaction to her "husband" that she'd spent not a moment thinking about how she would feel if her boss showed up with a beautiful woman on his arm. Now she knew exactly how it would feel—as if she'd been punched in the solar plexus.

So Spencer had a woman in his life. Then what was he doing making sheep's eyes at Jane? Unless she'd imagined it all and projected her own growing attraction onto him when all the time he viewed her only as a business associate? But even as the thought flitted through her brain she glanced at Spencer to find him looking at her. As their eyes met he turned to say something to his date, but not before Jane had seen the warmth in his gaze.

"Yumi, you've done a wonderful job organizing this," Jane said, forcing her gaze away from Spence and the statuesque redhead.

"Thanks. I like decorating. I had some trouble with the place cards, though. Couldn't find any I liked."

"Place cards?" Jane asked, seeing her plan to find a table tucked away in the back and sit with people she never saw day-to-day fade.

"Yep. I finally made cards on my computer. I put you at Spencer's table since you're new."

"Oh, you didn't have to do that. Really, I'd be more comfortable if—"

"It's all arranged. Can't change it now."

Spencer had finished whispering to his date and the last thing she wanted was for him to overhear her trying to dodge his company at dinner, so she smiled and assured Yumi she was delighted with the arrangements.

She wished she'd thought to pop a few pain relievers in her tiny clutch purse. Her head was starting to pound.

If sitting at the same table as Spencer and his bombshell date wasn't bad enough, she was seated directly across from Spence and his date was opposite Chuck. She tried to make small talk while mentally calculating how many hours of this torture she could expect before they could leave.

She'd forgotten Chuck was a fussy eater.

"What are you doing?" she whispered when she caught him with his nose almost touching the plate of antipasto that was put in front of him.

"I like to see what I'm eating," he grumbled.

"It's antipasto."

"What are the red things?"

"Grilled red peppers."

"I don't like red pepper."

"Eat the brown things. They're olives. You like olives." She felt as though she were negotiating with a two-year-old. Jane turned slightly and began talking to the computer engineer on her right. She wasn't aware the courses had changed until she heard a howl of pain from her left.

Chuck's nose emerged from the lobster bisque looking redder than the lobster itself.

It was too much to hope no one had noticed. She glanced up. Spencer was in the act of turning to his date, pretending he hadn't noticed Chuck wiping soup off his nose with his linen napkin.

Part of her wanted to strangle Chuck for being the worst date in the history of dating, but the decent part of her remembered that he was trying to help her out of a jam. Blinding him had been entirely her own fault.

"Are you okay, honey?" she said aloud, putting her arm around him and leaning in so she could whisper, "I'm sorry. You're being a true friend."

He turned to her and finally showed off his most attractive feature: his smile. "The things a man will do for the woman he loves." Even though she knew he referred to Alicia, she was still rather touched when he kissed her cheek. When she glanced up and found Spencer's gaze on her, at least she knew he'd seen genuine affection pass between her and Chuck.

When the main course arrived, Jane was ready. She whispered in Chuck's ear, "Lamb, six o'clock. Asparagus and hollandaise sauce nine o'clock. Roast potatoes, noon. Three o'clock, spinach...no never mind. I think that's red pepper with it."

"Got it. Thanks."

He seemed to be managing all right when Spencer leaned forward. "I understand you're interested in vampires, Chuck."

Damn. Her "husband" looked up vaguely. "Not unless they need their taxes done. I'm an accountant."

"In the entertainment industry," Jane added quickly.

"Jane, I never said I'd—"

A grunt of pain silenced him.

"He's very protective of his clients," she explained brightly. If she didn't feel so sorry for herself she might have some sympathy left over for poor Chuck. She was a rotten friend to put him through this. It wasn't his fault he was the date from hell.

Her headache escalated from pounding to the jackhammer stage.

She looked over at Spencer's dream date and, instead of reassuring her, the sight of the stunningly beautiful woman made her feel worse. Her eyes moved to her boss and she found his gaze on her, an inscrutable expression on his face. She felt her breath catch as she tried to think of something to say—something sociable and light.

There was chatter ebbing and flowing around them, a quartet playing background music, and she and Spence stared at each other silently as though each was unable, or unwilling, to break the spell.

It was broken rudely when she became aware that Chuck and the bombshell were having an animated conversation. He was telling her about his work as a senior tax expert, which had nothing whatsoever to do with the entertainment industry.

Two years of damned finishing school and she couldn't find a smooth way out of the worst social misadventure of her career.

"He does the taxes for movie stars," she claimed brightly.

Chuck might be persuaded to pose as his wife's friend's husband, but nothing in the world would make him take his work lightly. He shot Jane a reproving glance. "One theatrical animal handler. But most of my clients are business people."

"And what do you like to do in your spare time?" Chelsea asked.

He was going to mention bowling. She knew it and had to stop him before her pack of lies to Spencer were exposed. Frantically she tried to recall all the nonsense she'd spouted about poor Chuck's supposed hobbies. "Race-car driving," she said clearly, answering for him as though he were a shy child.

"That must be exciting," Chelsea said.

Chuck blinked slowly at Jane, then sighed. "You have no idea. My life gets more exciting every day."

He must have read the SOS signals in Jane's eyes for he took her hand. "Jane keeps my life interesting."

Fortunately, it was soon time for Spencer's State of the Union speech and the excruciating chitchat was forced to an end. Spence thanked the several hundred employees and their spouses for another great year and did some cheerleading as he inspired the troops for the coming months. He was articulate and amusing and Jane was finally able to relax, knowing that as soon as he finished, the dinner would officially be over and she and Chuck could leave without any further disasters.

Unless it could be counted as a disaster, when just as she and Chuck were about to leave Spencer appeared with her jacket, which she'd forgotten on the back of her chair. As he slipped it on her shoulders his fingertips brushed her bare shoulder and the tremors went right to her toes.

"See you Monday, Jane," he said.

SPENCER'S SILVER BMW purred through the streets. Beside him Chelsea flicked through his CDs.

"Thanks for coming tonight," Spencer said as the first strains of jazz floated through the car.

"You're welcome. Thanks for inviting me. I needed to get out. Lately I've been spending time only with students or myself."

He loosened his bow tie. "Yeah."

Chelsea glanced at him curiously but didn't say anything.

"If you're sitting around the house moping while that SOB you married is off on the other side of the world digging up rotting dinosaur bones then you're not the woman I took you for."

"I'd like to remind you that that SOB is your brother and no, I'm not moping. I go out with my women friends, but I miss evenings out with him." She sighed deeply. "I just miss him."

Spencer nodded. He knew what it was like to long for the simple things about married life. Like someone to come home to at night. Chelsea could have gone with her husband on his six-month dig, but she loved her job as a psychology professor at the university as much as Bill loved poring through sand and dirt looking for old bones. So they paid the price of missing each other for long stretches of time.

"I hope he knows how lucky he is." Spencer thought about Karen. Apart from business trips, which he always kept as short as possible, he'd lived in town the whole of their marriage, but she'd still gone off and had an affair, while Bill traveled for months at a time and Chelsea waited patiently—and celibately—until he returned.

"I hope he does, too," she said. "It's a strange marriage, I guess, but it works for us." Her tone was wistful, despite her words. He would have pursued the subject, but she changed it to one of much more interest to him. "Speaking of strange marriages, what was with Chuck and Jane?"

He'd been wondering the same thing, and he was glad Chelsea had raised the subject. "What do you mean?"

"I mean they're an odd couple."

"Well, he did seem a little uncoordinated."

Chelsea's rich laugh echoed. "Uncoordinated? The man couldn't see! He told me his wife made him come tonight, and he didn't look happy about it. He had a glasses case sticking out of his pocket, but when I asked him about it he said Jane wouldn't let him wear them. What's that about?"

Spence was at least as stumped as Chelsea. Jane had treated Chuck more like a pet than a husband. "I guess there's no accounting for tastes."

They were cruising the tree-lined avenues near the university. The yellowing leaves were gilded by the car's headlights. Spencer slowed to a stop in front of Chelsea's house, leaving the engine running.

"I enjoyed myself. Thanks for the pity date," his companion said, her hand resting lightly on the door handle.

"You were the one who took pity on me so I wouldn't have to go stag. Thanks."

He waited until she was safely inside and had flipped on a couple of lights and waved from the living-room window before he headed home.

If he were completely truthful, he hadn't simply been giving a work-widow a night out. He hadn't wanted to be at a disadvantage with Jane. If she was going to bring the handsome husband she'd raved about, he was going to display an attractive woman on his arm. Fair was fair.

He shook his head in the darkness of the car as a clarinet crooned the blues from his CD player. It was some comfort to know that Chelsea's impressions matched his. He'd heard love was blind but this one was also deaf and dumb. He'd never seen a more mismatched couple than Jane and Chuck. It wasn't merely that she was gorgeous while he was...well, not. It was how little they seemed to have in common.

They didn't even know each other. Spencer remembered his conversation with Jane in the airport clearly. He'd made himself concentrate as she listed her husband's hobbies. He needed to paint a picture in his imagination of a real man who could be badly hurt if a latent attraction between his wife and her co-worker got out of hand. But she'd made Chuck sound like a cross between Adonis and a superhero—nothing like any man he knew.

The real Chuck reminded him of a cartoon character, all right—not a superhero, but a goofy nerd. Spencer was still trying to puzzle it out as he pulled into his underground parking stall, but it was a puzzle he couldn't solve.

All he knew was that the most interesting woman he'd met in a very long time was taken.

Whatever he wished, or felt, he couldn't change that. He'd better spend his energy thinking of Jane Stanford as one of the sales team—like Mike or Brent or Yoshi. His snort echoed off the cement walls of the empty parking garage. Yeah, that was going to happen.

5

SPENCER AWOKE to find that even though it was the weekend, the sun had decided to stick around. Most unusual. The light was brilliant, but, as he stepped out on his balcony, he felt a hint of fall in the air. His apartment looked out over English Bay and below him, along the seaside path, he watched countless joggers, inline skaters, bikers, stroller-pushing parents, even an enterprising popcorn vendor. All of Vancouver seemed to be out enjoying nature's last burst of summer.

He showered quickly and brewed some coffee. He had work to catch up on this weekend, but the sun drew him. The rainy season would be setting in soon, he told himself. He could work then. On impulse, he picked up the phone, called Chelsea and invited her to go blading with him in Stanley Park.

She'd sounded less than thrilled with the latest work separation from Bill, and Spence wouldn't be much of a brother-in-law if he didn't give her a sympathetic ear.

Within an hour, he and Chelsea were skating along a crowded seawall sharing their lane with cyclists, a gaggle of baby carriages, even a stubborn Canada goose who stood in the middle of the path hissing.

The ocean lapped contentedly against the stone wall, tossing up the scent of seaweed. Spencer let his thoughts float as aimlessly as the ducks bobbing on the water below. He thought about the company party the night before and shook his helmeted head in puzzlement.

He'd been so sure meeting Jane's husband would be a smart thing to do. But that was before he met him. Now, on top of his inconvenient infatuation with an employee, he had the added burden of worrying that her marriage was a mistake.

She didn't even seem to know the guy, he thought again, recalling how their descriptions of Chuck's career hadn't exactly coincided. Spencer thought about that for a minute, skating to the left to skirt round a couple who were giving each other tonsillectomies on wheels. Now that guy had love in his eyes. Chuck looked at Jane more the way a hunted fox might regard the baying hounds closing in on him.

He tried to shrug off his impressions. Jane was a big girl. She must have married the guy for her own reasons. For all he knew Chuck was shy and always acted that skittish around strangers.

It was a gorgeous day, and he'd be seeing Jane tomorrow. There was no point in worrying about her marriage today. She was probably miles away thinking of anything but him.

"I CAN'T BELIEVE you talked me into this," Jane protested as she wobbled over to Alicia on rented inline skates that felt terrifyingly unstable.

"It's a beautiful day and we need the exercise. Besides, I want to hear about last night without a lot of additional comments on my failings as a wife thrown in."

Jane glanced back at Chuck, fiddling with the straps on his safety helmet. "Has he been giving you a hard time?"

Alicia twirled around a couple of times and Jane belatedly remembered she'd been a provincial junior ice-skating champion in high school. "Not as bad as the time I made him dress in drag for that AIDS fund-raiser."

Jane suppressed a giggle. "Why does he let you do these things to him?"

Alicia winked. "Because he loves me."

Jane felt a funny pang. From anyone else the statement might have sounded arrogant, but with Alicia and Chuck it was the simple truth. A marriage like that...

What was she thinking about? She'd gone to a lot of trouble to avoid marriage, consciously deciding to put her career first. A little crush on a certain someone was no reason to toss away the years of work she'd put into building her future.

Mr. Nobody was the perfect bridegroom and she planned to be faithful to him.

Still... She watched Alicia glide effortlessly on her skates over to where Chuck was making an effort to stay upright on his, pulling himself from tree-branch to tree-branch in a tottering, undignified manner.

Alicia took his hand and they began skating together. Chuck would drive most women to drink before the honeymoon was over, but he had something Alicia needed. He was the rock who anchored her exuberant friend. And Alicia brought all the excitement into his life Chuck would ever need.

She bit her lip as she considered some of the crazy things poor Chuck had been dragged into thanks to Alicia. Including last night's less-than-brilliant acting job. She'd thanked him with true gratitude, but she knew he never would have pretended to be her husband if Alicia hadn't talked him into it. Yes, he must really love his wife.

"Carry on down that track, Jane," her friend called out as she helped her husband onto the bumpy asphalt. "It meets up with the main path. We'll catch up."

Jane took a deep breath. The narrow snake of pavement seemed harmless. Also, it was deserted, which would give her a few minutes to practice. She'd been on roller skates when she was a kid, but they'd had about six wide wheels and felt like shoes. These roller blades were more like ice skates. Jane had never been much of a skater.

But she was padded, helmeted, and in reasonable shape. How bad could it be?

In less than a minute she had the answer to her question. It could be bad. Very, very bad.

The innocent-looking path began to tilt downward.

Like a cat skidding across a freshly waxed floor, Jane stuck her arms and legs out rigidly in front of her and suddenly realized she'd forgotten to ask Alicia how to stop. Frantically, she tried to figure it out for herself. She could see the Stanley Park seawall now, swarming with people, all of whom seemed to be in perfect control of whatever wheeled device they were operating.

She heard Alicia shout something behind her, but the words wouldn't penetrate her panic-stricken brain.

Snowplowing didn't stop her, and just about sent her sprawling. She tried Chuck's trick of grabbing at tree branches, but they were out of reach.

With a terrified whimper she closed her eyes.

She blasted onto the main path, which was at least flat, but now she had to maneuver through the Sunday crowds. "Help, sorry, 'scuse me..." she called out as she swung wildly left and right, narrowly avoiding collisions. She knew it was only a matter of time till she went sprawling, but she hung on grimly.

She spotted two skaters ahead of her, both in perfect form, looking as though they'd been born on the damn blades.

"How do you stop these things?" she cried out as she careened by the couple.

"Jane?" She heard the surprise in the oh-so familiar voice.

"Spencer, thank God. Help me!" she shouted into the wind, unable to turn around.

Horrified, she saw that she was closing in on side-by-side baby carriages, and there was no room to get around them. There was nothing for it. She couldn't flatten a pair of infants. She'd have to throw herself to the ground.

One minute Spencer was behind her, and then, just as she prepared to sacrifice her dignity and her limbs to protect innocent babies, his dark shape zoomed past her and he turned to face her, holding his arms out.

Didn't he get it? "Look out, I can't stop." She tried snowplowing again, anything to stop herself from rolling right over her boss, but he just stood there like a punching bag.

With no room to hit the ground, she thumped into him. She heard him grunt but his strong arms came blessedly around her and he was skating backward. She hadn't flattened him. Instead he'd taken her impact and kept moving, slowing them both down.

She was clinging to him, her face plastered to his chest, her arms wrapped tightly around his torso, which felt altogether too good—safe and comforting. He even smelled good. Clean and healthy and male.

"You didn't let me fall," she mumbled into his cotton T-shirt.

"Of course not." He squeezed her in a light hug. "You can trust me." When the world finally stopped moving and she felt her heart slow its frantic pounding, she looked up. His eyes were crinkled at the corners, his cheeks creased in a smile. His arms were looped behind her and he felt so warm and solid, she never wanted to let go. In fact, she wanted to collapse against his chest again and stay like that for a good week or two.

She'd only ever seen Spencer in business attire. Today he wore black running shorts that revealed powerful thighs, and a gray Canucks T-shirt that had seen better days. He looked relaxed, fit and frankly amused.

"Thanks," she managed to croak.

"Remind me to check our life-insurance and accident policy tomorrow. I'm not sure we can afford you."

Jane was suddenly aware that she was being stared

at, and turned to see a familiar statuesque redhead looking at her with unabashed curiosity.

As if it weren't bad enough that she should make a complete fool of herself in front of Spencer, she had to do so in front of Red, as well. This was one weekend she'd never forget.

Spencer turned, following the direction of her gaze, keeping one arm casually around Jane's waist.

"You remember Chelsea?"

"Yes. Hello again."

"Jane, are you all right?" Alicia came to a smooth stop in front of Jane, dragging the hapless Chuck by the hand.

His stop was less smooth. Had it not been for the shin-high rock wall he would have joined the ducks paddling placidly in the water below. Even though his knee-pads hit the wall and stopped his progress, his upper body still kept moving in the direction of the ocean. Jane grabbed his other arm, and between them, she and Alicia hauled him back, which at least gave her a graceful way to escape the too-wonderful feel of Spencer's arm tucked around her waist.

Chuck sat on the wall, a mulish look on his face. He shoved his thick glasses back up his nose and squinted until he found his wife.

"That is it, Alicia." He leaned forward and began unlacing his skates. "All I wanted to do was go for a walk. After the weekend I've had, is that too much to ask? I've been gussied up, dragged around, forced to pretend I'm...aaagh!"

"Sorry." Jane smiled brightly and pulled herself up after the accidental-on-purpose slip that had knocked

Chuck's feet out from under him. Unfortunately, her hip had connected with the paved seawall. She tried not to wince as she rose, rubbing her hip bone.

"Uh, Chuck, honey. You remember Spencer Tate, my *boss*? And his friend Chelsea? We met them last night." She spoke the words to Chuck but made sure they were loud enough for Alicia to hear.

Chuck looked long and hard at Spencer through his thick glasses, as though he were seeing him for the first time, which, come to think of it, he probably was.

Alicia made a choking sound, then stuck out her hand to shake first Chelsea's, then Spencer's. "Hi, I'm Alicia. Alicia, uh, Sorenson. I'm a friend of Jane's and Chuck's. In fact I was just looking after him for her. Helping him with the skates." Her smile was getting so big it looked as though it was about to swallow the rest of her face.

Jane sank shakily beside Chuck who was back to mumbling to his boots. She heard the words *bigamist*, and *lunatic* and there was a long rambling sentence where *that woman* figured prominently. She wasn't sure whether it was herself or Alicia he was referring to, but she prayed Spencer couldn't hear him.

When Alicia finally quit babbling about what a nice day it was, Jane fixed an over bright smile on her own face. "Well, nice to see you Spencer. Thanks for saving me from disaster. Nice to see you again, Chelsea."

"Yes, you too," the other woman said with a polite nod before skating expertly back to Spencer's side.

Spencer, however, seemed in no hurry to move.

There was an odd expression on his face. "Chelsea and I were just going to grab a coffee. Care to join us?"

"Oh, no. Thanks anyway, we've—"

"Coffee would be good," Chuck said firmly. "My feet are pinched in these damn things."

Jane wished she hadn't hauled him back from the brink of a cold swim with the ducks. She should have let him enjoy a frigid soak in the sea. She threw a panicked look at Alicia who seemed to have lost her wits and could only stand there with that inane smile glued to her face. "Well, Jane. Your *husband* wants coffee."

"Alicia, what are you—"

Just as Jane was preparing to throw herself to the hard ground again to shut Chuck up, he heaved a long-suffering sigh and shook his head. "Oh, no," he said.

Alicia skated forward to the rescue, deliberately misunderstanding him. "Come on Chuck, it's not that far to the snack bar. Jane and I will both help you."

And so each woman grabbed one of Chuck's arms and dragged him to the snack bar, a bit like a pair of tough cops hauling a criminal to jail.

Chuck seemed to realize escape was hopeless, but he kept up a muttering monologue all the way. Jane telegraphed urgent messages to Alicia from over his bent head, but Alicia merely shrugged as if to say, "What can I do?"

Spencer and his date skated off ahead, looking smooth and confident. If they'd left the party together last night and were now blading together in the morning, Jane thought, this wasn't the only exercise they'd undertaken in the last twelve hours.

Not that it was any of her business. In fact, she'd rather not have known. And that strange feeling in the pit of her stomach must be hunger. She certainly had no right to feel disappointment, or, heaven forbid, jealousy.

She, as Alicia was so fond of reminding her, had made her own bed and now she had to lie in it. Unfortunately, it was starting to feel like a bed of nails.

By the time Jane, Chuck and Alicia lurched, staggered and swayed up to the snack area, Chelsea was sitting alone at a picnic table and Spencer was coming toward them with a take-out tray of steaming paper cups.

Despite the fact that she now knew he had a woman in his life, Jane couldn't help the way her mouth dried when he approached. It was awareness of him as a man. The kind of man who looks as at home in the athletic arena as he does in the business one. Now that she'd seen him with another woman, she realized how much she wanted to get to know him herself. She sighed bitterly. She'd blown this one, but good.

He seemed to feel her gaze and, through the steam coming off the cups, his eyes met hers.

She swallowed, feeling suddenly breathless. Then Spencer broke eye contact to address Chuck. "Takes some getting used to, doesn't it?"

Chuck looked from Jane to Alicia and back again. He opened his mouth to speak but whatever he was going to say didn't emerge. Alicia jumped in before he had a chance. "Oh, I know. I think inline skating is a lot harder than it looks."

Spencer put coffees in front of everyone and pushed a pile of creamers, sugar packets and stir sticks into the middle of the table. He also had a paper plate with half a dozen Danish pastries on it.

While they all fixed their coffees Jane concentrated on finding a way out of this latest disaster.

Gulping coffee at record speed to get away as soon as possible was the only idea she could come up with. She'd end up with a burned mouth, but that was nothing compared to the torture of sitting here with her "husband" and Spencer's girlfriend.

Alicia helped herself to a Danish. "Mmm. Thanks. I'm starving." Seagulls had spotted the food and were wheeling overhead or pacing in the vicinity of the picnic table, black staring eyes glued to the pastries. A couple of crows got into a tussle over an abandoned sandwich bag at an empty table nearby.

"I missed breakfast," said Chelsea biting into her own Danish.

Jane followed suit when Spence offered her the plate. She'd eaten breakfast and was too busy feeling stressed out by this chance encounter to be hungry, but the quicker they downed the food and drink, the quicker they'd be out of here.

She took a second Danish and plonked it in front of Chuck, her pathetic strategy being that if she could keep his mouth full, he couldn't get the pair of them into any more trouble with his inappropriate comments. Besides, she thought the gesture looked wifely.

Chelsea and Alicia hit it off and were soon swapping skating stories. Chelsea was warm and funny, and even though she was sleeping with Spence, Jane couldn't help but like her.

"Did it take you very long to get the hang of these things?" Jane asked her, pointing to the inline skates.

"Spencer's brother bought them for me and then took me out blading until I got good enough not to embarrass him. It's fun."

Jane could have cared less about how much fun Chelsea had on inline skates. She was much more interested in the identity of the skate purchaser. "You know Spencer's brother?"

Chelsea grinned. "I'm married to him."

"You're married to Spencer's *brother?*" So she wasn't his girlfriend. Which meant...

"He's on a dig in Africa. Spence takes pity on me sometimes and gets me out of the house."

"That's nice," Jane said mechanically. She shot a glance at Spencer and found him looking irritated. Now why...

Unless he'd wanted her, Jane, to think he was seeing someone.

And why would he care about that unless he...

The sun was feeling warmer than it had any right to in September and she decided she liked Chelsea better all the time. "Don't you miss him?" she asked, thinking if the brother was anything like Spence, it would be torture to be separated.

A shadow crossed Chelsea's face. "Yes. I miss him a lot. But I have my own work and can't just pick up and leave at my husband's whim."

Uh-oh. Something told her all was not well in in-law

land. None of her business, she thought. She may have had a momentary lapse of finishing-school etiquette, but she was back on track now. Instead of prying into a marriage that was no concern of hers, she asked what kind of work Chelsea did.

"I'm a psychology professor at UBC," she said. "That's how I met Spence's brother. He teaches there, too. When he's in the country." There could be no mistaking the dry tone of the last sentence. Chelsea was ticked at her husband for leaving her for months at a time.

Jane didn't blame her a bit for her annoyance. That's what happened when dedicated career women got married. They were expected to put their lives on hold at the whim of their husband's careers. She'd seen it happen too many times. At least Chelsea wasn't sacrificing her own career to run after her husband. She was a woman after Jane's own heart.

The last Danish sat there, its lemon center glinting in the sun and she saw Alicia eyeing it. The woman was always eating. "Does anyone want that last pastry?" Alicia finally asked.

There was general head shaking. Chelsea said, "I'm trying to lose a couple of pounds. Too much time at the computer and not enough exercise." She wrinkled her nose. "I hate diets."

"Ugh," Alicia said. "I never diet. Tried it once and I gained weight. I'm lucky, I think. I have a good metabolism." Her white teeth sank, with obvious enjoyment, into the Danish.

Jane glanced quickly around. They all seemed to be

done with their coffees. As soon as Alicia downed that Danish, they'd be on their way. She was just congratulating herself on muddling through an awkward situation when Chuck leaned over to Alicia and kissed her cheek. For once he wasn't mumbling.

"I'm glad you don't diet," he said. "I think your body is sexy as hell."

6

WHAT WAS the matter with Jane's husband?

Spencer was still trying to figure it out as he crunched numbers to make the Holt Marsden deal even sweeter. He heard an unusual amount of Monday-morning buzzing outside the door as his staff rehashed Saturday night's party. From what he could overhear, it seemed everyone had had a good time.

Everyone but him.

His plan had backfired.

Instead of finding Jane happily married to a guy he liked, he'd discovered that she and her husband were an odd couple to say the least.

His impression hadn't changed in the park yesterday. He shook his head at the memory of Chuck ogling Jane's best friend right under her nose. When he'd told Alicia she had a sexy body, Spencer didn't know who at the table had been more shocked, there were so many gaping mouths and red faces.

The strangest thing was that Alicia was an attractive woman, while Jane was a beauty.

A ten, a man-killer, a babe.

For all the trouble she invested in playing down her looks, he had seldom seen a more beautiful woman.

Chuck was the classic ninety-eight-pound weakling

who had scored the bombshell. He must be certifiably nuts to let his myopic gaze wander.

Shaking his head, Spence recalled how gorgeous Jane had looked even in a pair of jeans and a purple sweater. He relived those moments of holding her on the seawall while she'd looked up at him, her cheeks flushed. He'd wanted to kiss her as she glanced up at him, half shy and half laughing.

He gritted his teeth in frustration. If *he* was married to Jane he would never even look at another woman.

And that was his biggest problem.

He wasn't married to her, and Chuck was.

The mega-babe, the bombshell in pin-stripes who was starting to appear in his dreams, sleeping as well as waking—was taken, married, unavailable. She could never be his. It didn't matter how worthless and undeserving her husband was. She had chosen him, and Spence had to accept it.

He and Jane worked together. That was it.

Over the next few days, however, Spence began to wonder if they did work together anymore. He never saw his newest sales manager.

He'd become accustomed to seeing her each day as she walked by his open door on the way to her own office. Now she was either coming in earlier than he was, or walking a circuitous route through accounting to avoid him.

He wondered if she was embarrassed about her husband's behavior. Probably.

He was sure as hell embarrassed by it.

He missed her, though. Even if it was just a brief greeting as they passed in the hall, or an even briefer glimpse of her as she headed past his open door. Well, Jane couldn't avoid him forever. Meetings were a way of life at Datatracker.

Until the next one, he would respect that she wanted to avoid him. The less time they spent together, the better for everyone.

Unfortunately, he saw Jane even when he didn't see her. He'd be staring at his computer screen and instead of words and numbers Jane would appear, as she'd been on the seawall, her arms thrown around him, leaning into him for balance. Her delicately-flushed face would be laughing up into his, her blue eyes gleaming.

He'd wake in the night, a smile still on his lips and his body aching for the woman who was just out of his reach. He'd groan as the reality struck. She belonged to another man.

He had it bad. Here he was lusting after a co-worker just like that SOB at Graham's.

He'd been keeping his relationships with women as casual as possible for the past couple of years, partly because he was bitter over his divorce and partly because he was just so damned busy at work. By the time he'd think about calling someone, it was usually too late to go out.

But the old libido was definitely looking for some action. Hell, he was a healthy man in the prime of his life. Probably, the thing with Jane could easily be replaced by a woman who was actually available. He needed some female companionship and some sex. That's what his dreams were telling him.

Even if he didn't come into contact with Jane every

day, he knew she was on the premises. He'd pass her car, or see a memo with her name on it. That's why he was starting to think about her too much, he thought, and in the wrong context. There was a perfectly simple solution to his problem. He needed a new outlet for his attention.

He needed a woman.

One day, after a particularly erotic vision, he pulled out his electronic notebook—the little black book of the twenty-first century. In it was a file containing the names of information on women he dated from time to time—fun women who weren't looking for white picket fences any more than he was.

The file was password-protected. He realized he hadn't been out in a while when he couldn't immediately remember how to get into it. What was the damned password? He looked down at the small blinking curser in frustration, then remembered. He entered ZENA.

Spencer liked to be aggressive when he planned a strategy, whether business or personal. So, having decided he needed some female companionship to turf Jane out of his fantasies, he made three dates with three different women over the next week.

With a pleasant sense of having accomplished something worthwhile he finished tweaking his notes on the Marsden deal and e-mailed them to Jane. If she wanted to play it cool, he could do the same.

Once that was sent, he took a break from his computer to check on the prototype of a new device in the Datatracker family. He deserved a treat.

He wandered down the hallway and down a flight

of stairs, greeting everyone he passed, pausing to swap jokes and chat briefly. He made a point of getting out and mingling with the staff on a daily basis. He learned things he'd never find out sitting behind his desk all day, and the casual interaction gave staffers a chance to ask questions or talk to him in an informal way. Maybe they didn't teach his management style at Harvard, but it worked for Spence.

Computer Engineering was a labyrinthine maze of cubicles that probably held more brilliant but eccentric brain cells per square inch than a top university. The department's sign was plastered over with a computer printout renaming the place in code, but anyone could have instantly identified the section upon seeing or hearing a staff member. Here techno-nerds ruled supreme.

These were Spencer's people. And this was the department he loved most of all.

As he neared, Spencer felt his heart quicken with excitement, and not only because he was about to visit the latest Datatracker baby.

Jane was standing just outside. She had on a gray pantsuit and flat shoes. Her hair was neatly styled in a French braid.

The outfit was about as sexy as a potato sack. Spencer felt heat rush straight to his groin.

"Here to see the new baby?" he asked from behind her. Jane jumped at the sound of his voice. As she turned quickly to glance at him, he caught a blush in her cheeks. He smelled her almond shampoo and let himself just enjoy looking at her for a minute.

"That's right. I came to take a peek at the prototype for the new RDT-240."

"Me, too. Come on."

Jane looked as though she would refuse and he raised his eyebrows in a silent challenge. So he thought she was gorgeous and sexy. What did she think he was going to do to her? He could control himself. If he tried very, very hard.

She must have realized it would look as if she was running away if she turned around now, so she raised her chin slightly and looked him right in the eye. "Lead on."

The RDT-240, the newest in Datatracker's line was a creation only an engineer could love. Spencer loved it. He looked into its innards, its heart, guts and brain, and felt a parental surge of pride. The intricate arrangement of circuit boards and chips was as individual as DNA. Of course, as with the birth of any infant, there had been labor pains.

He asked about a few glitches the team was ironing out and felt his hands itch to dig in and get involved. He missed being part of the creation. Even though he knew he was good at being CEO of the company, he also knew that the board of venture capitalists who had financed his firm had promoted him out of the job he loved.

Jane didn't love the RDT-240. But she would have to sell it. He watched her try and keep up with the techno-babble.

After half an hour or so, Eddie, an engineer who'd been with the company almost as long as Spencer had and was the unofficial head of the department, motioned for them to follow him into his cubicle at the end of a corridor.

Spence trailed Jane into the small space which smelled like Old Spice and wet gym socks. It was so crowded with computer equipment, whiteboard and racquetball paraphernalia that he and Jane ended up shoulder to shoulder wedged between a duffel bag, from which the wet-sock smell seemed to emanate, and the paper-covered wall.

Eddie's freckled face twisted in an infantile grin. "I don't want to spoil the young guys' fun, but I think I fixed that glitch in the prototype."

Spencer felt as if his only son had scored his first touchdown. "You're sure?"

"I'm testing it this afternoon, but I think so." Eddie explained what he'd done, all too eager to have the ear of a fellow geek who could appreciate his talents. Spencer did. His fingers damned near itched to get involved. Barely aware that he was doing it, he loosened his tie.

He almost forgot Jane was standing there until she moved slightly, and suddenly he realized they'd been boring her senseless. He glanced up to apologize and found her gazing at him with tolerant amusement.

"You really love this stuff don't you?"

He nodded with a wry grin and turned back to Eddie. "Maybe I could spare some time this afternoon to help test—" But even as the idea occurred to him he had to reject it. He was wearing the damn tie for a reason. He had a meeting this afternoon with the venture capital firm that had given Datatracker its start.

He'd have to play with the big boys, when he'd much rather muck about in the sandbox with the tykes.

The only bright spot in his afternoon was that he'd asked Jane to join them. He'd wanted the venture capital people to get to know her. She'd be giving a presentation on the deals they were currently working on, and besides, she had the kind of sharp mind about details and figures that those finance guys loved.

She'd told him at their first meeting that she was ambitious and he'd believed her. Luckily for both of them, she was also smart, talented and organized. He had a strong feeling she'd be moving up in the company and the fellows at this afternoon's meeting would be good to have onside.

He'd be bored out of his gourd, but at least Jane would be there.

As he'd suspected, the venture capital guys were a lot more interested in the markets, profit potential and shipping schedule for the RDT-240 than they were in its design and circuitry.

He turned over a lot of the meeting to Jane and she both charmed the venture capitalists and spoke to them in their own language.

She also charmed the hell out of Spencer.

When the meeting broke up, the venture capital guys left as they'd arrived, in a clump. It was close to seven, so only a few diehards were still at work in cubicles or offices. Where Spence and Jane were usually surrounded by people, now the Datatracker building felt quiet and intimate.

They walked out together and he heard her heels

echo on the floor as he complimented her on the way she'd handled herself in the meeting.

She chuckled. "I merely gave them the kind of figures they like to see."

If she didn't realize what a double entendre that was, he wasn't going to enlighten her. In fact, she had the kind of figure all men like to see, and Spencer was certainly no exception. His inner male animal was currently growling and pawing the ground with frustrated yearning.

It had rained earlier, and dark oily-looking blobs turned out to be puddles in the dips of the outside parking lot. A damp chill hovered in the air and he was so attuned to Jane he sensed her shiver.

He knew he ought to leave her and turn toward his own vehicle, but he couldn't make his feet obey his brain. No surprise there. He couldn't make most of his body obey his brain when Jane was around.

He did manage to keep his conversation centered on that meeting, even though his thoughts were elsewhere. They chatted of business things while their bodies hummed to an entirely personal frequency. They made it to her dark blue Volvo and she slipped her keys out of her bag.

"How do you do that?" he asked her, amazed.

She turned to him in surprise. "Do what?"

"That thing with your keys? Do you have some kind of psychic power? You reached into that bag and pulled them out. It takes me about ten minutes to find my keys, and I don't carry a big bag with a bunch of makeup and things in it."

Her glorious blue eyes were twinkling, extra sparkle

thrown in by the exterior lights that rimmed the perimeter of the parking area. "I always put them in the same inner pocket of my bag, so I know where they are."

"Oh, right. Must be a girl thing."

"Girl thing?"

Even as she stared at him, he realized that wasn't true. "No, wait. I've seen lots of women fumble for their keys. Karen, my ex-wife, used to get so frustrated she'd dump her purse upside down, wherever she happened to be. Parking garage, side of the road, it didn't matter." He shook his head. "Used to irritate the hell out of me, but I'm just as bad."

"It's simple enough to keep them organized. Pick a place and always put your keys in the same spot," she said as though he were a very dimwitted kindergartner.

"Right. Sure."

She glanced at him from under her lashes, leaning back slightly against her car. "So, where are your keys now?"

He wished he'd never said a word. If she hadn't made hers appear like magic, he wouldn't have. He shoved his hands in his suit pockets and felt around. No. No keys. Not in the trouser pockets. Not in the jacket pockets. He'd been half joking when he teased her about her organization, but it wasn't all that funny when he was standing here as though he had a bad case of hives, slapping all over his body as he tried to feel for the jagged lump of his keys.

"I should have kept my mouth shut. They're here. Somewhere." He even patted his back pockets, though if they'd been there he'd have known that when he sat down.

It was too warm for an overcoat, but had he started out with one and left the keys in the pocket? Or were they on his desk?

He didn't think so.

They must be in his briefcase. He dug around in there and sure enough, they were at the very bottom. With a grunt of triumph, he pulled them out, the silver glinting in the light from the street lamp—almost as blinding as the light from her teeth as she laughed at him.

"Think it's funny, huh?" he said, closing in with a menacing growl. She was so gorgeous, so irresistible that he forgot himself for a moment—just long enough for his inner animal to slip its leash.

He moved closer until his thighs brushed hers and his face was inches above her own. Passion flickered in her eyes and her lips parted in a soft sigh as he closed the distance between them.

He raised a hand and laid it against her cheek, finding it just as velvety soft as he'd guessed it would be. A tiny sigh escaped her lips and he felt the way her head tilted, making her mouth more accessible to him.

That wasn't an invitation he was going to turn down.

His own eyes closed as he prepared to kiss the lips that had been driving him crazy with desire for weeks.

But he didn't make it.

A small, firm hand on his chest stopped him in mid pucker. "Spencer, don't."

A bucket of ice cubes dumped on his head couldn't have shocked him more.

Her voice was husky, and he heard as well as felt her own desire. But she, at least, had some morals. And a little self-control. She'd stopped him before he did the one thing he most wanted to do, and the thing he'd most regret. For if he kissed her senseless as he was yearning to do, he'd then do his utmost to get her into bed.

Horrified at what he'd almost done, he leapt back.

"Jane, I'm sorry. I didn't mean— Oh, hell. I did mean...but I don't want you to think..."

While he babbled, she quietly unlocked and opened her car. She might look as composed as usual, but he could see her hand trembling.

"Please, don't say any more. It's my fault." She wouldn't look at him as she slid into the car.

He grabbed the door before she could shut it. "It's no one's fault. But we have to talk about what's going on. We've got to—"

"There's nothing going on. Nothing."

She might believe those words, but her inner wild woman had come out to play with his inner wild man. It had been only for a minute, but that was long enough for Spencer to conclude that she was as racked with desire as he was.

And what the hell were they going to do about it?

7

"WHAT AM I going to do?" Jane wailed to Alicia. They were curled up on her friend's couch, an empty wine bottle on the floor between them.

The wine hadn't eased her utter confusion a single bit. If anything, she felt worse.

"Alicia," she repeated, "what am I going to do? I was a heartbeat away from kissing him, and I have an awful feeling it wouldn't have stopped at kissing."

There was a disturbing twinkle in her friend's eye. "Call the podiatrist. That guy's got your toes so curled you walk like a vulture. It's not pretty."

"All right, all right. You told me so. I should have listened and never come up with such a crazy idea. I was so arrogant. All I thought about was guys I wasn't interested in making passes at me. I never thought I might meet a guy I wanted."

Alicia reached for a handful of nuts. "Could it be time to ask Tom Cruise for a divorce?"

"Very funny," she snapped. "And where would that leave me?"

"Free to make a pass at your extremely sexy boss, that's where." Alicia munched her peanuts, then drained her glass.

Jane felt her blood pressure rise as she contemplated doing what Alicia suggested. "Oh, yes. That's a good idea. Then what will I be? The woman who got ahead by sleeping with the boss? I don't think so. Sex and the workplace don't mix."

Alicia snorted. "Then you should be looking for work in a nunnery or an all-girls' school. Get with it, woman. I'll bet half the couples I know met through work. You're allowed to be human in the workplace."

"Then how come I got fired from Graham's?"

Alicia gaped at her. "The two situations are nothing alike. What happened with Johnson was a clear case of sexual harassment. Which reminds me, I wanted to tell you that all of us women had a meeting after you left. We're getting together with the director of human resources to formulate a sexual-harassment policy. Johnson had better watch out. What happened to you will never happen again if I can help it."

Jane's anger dimmed as she smiled at her friend. "Good for you."

"But it's different with you and Spencer. What you feel is mutual, healthy attraction."

"Hmmph. For now. And if we have an affair and it doesn't work out who will be the one who has to leave the company? The president or the newest of six salespeople?"

"So what? He's your ideal man. Is a job more important?"

"It's not just a job to me. It's my career."

Alicia shook her head, her curls bobbing. "Sometimes I'd like to go beat up those parents of yours."

"What are you talking about? They would agree with everything you're saying."

Those curls quivered again, this time in denial.

"They want you to marry the right man for all the wrong reasons. I'm telling you to go for the wrong man for all the right reasons."

"I don't get it."

"Now there's a news flash. And that's another one of your problems."

"Sex has nothing to do with this," Jane snapped. If there was anything that irritated her it was married women who pitied her for her sexless state. Big deal. In her opinion the whole thing was overrated anyway.

"Sex has everything to do with it." Alicia sighed. "Let's get some dinner on before Chuck gets home and threatens to call A.A. again."

Jane grinned. "We might have to call the paramedics if Chuck gets home and sees me here. He's starting to hate the sight of me."

"Don't be silly. He loves you." Alicia dimpled. "He just doesn't want to be married to you. Stay. I think we need to work on a strategy for you."

Jane's irritation dissipated and she smiled at her friend. "It's pretty obvious you're the one he loves having for a wife."

Alicia grinned again. "In spite of all the trouble I get him into we're celebrating five years next week."

"Five years? I can't believe it's been that long." She'd been a bridesmaid at their wedding and it felt like months ago rather than years. An odd pang shot through her. Was she getting old? She'd always vaguely planned to get married someday, after her career was established, but if she kept letting her life slide by in five-year increments, she'd still be alone when she collected her gold watch and pension.

Alicia nodded. "I've talked the cheapskate into taking me to dinner at Il Paradiso."

"Does he have any idea what the prices are like?"

Alicia chuckled. "I told him if he orders the house wine, the marriage is off."

They hauled off the couch and made their way to the kitchen to put some dinner together. Alicia always had a well-stocked kitchen and Jane was in the habit of eating over every couple of weeks or so. It wasn't fancy, which was part of the charm. Alicia was like the sister she'd never had.

As they worked together in the kitchen Alicia asked, over the hiss of the frying pan, "So, if you're not going to be sensible and get a divorce, what are you going to do?"

The knife in Jane's hand stilled. The scent of onion tickling the back of her nose made her feel like crying. "I don't know. I want to give Spencer the Marsden Holt account. It means a lot to him, and frankly..." She paused and automatically neatened the chopped heap of onion slices. "Well, I know revenge is petty, but I want to win that account back for my own satisfaction as well."

"Another black eye for Johnson?"

"Something like that." Jane took a resolute breath. "I'm thinking of asking Marsden Holt for a job."

Alicia turned around. "What? But they don't even have an office here."

"That's right. I'd have to move to Detroit. A green card's no problem. I was born in Boston."

"But this is your home—your friends are here."

"I feel like I need a new start."

"And Spencer?"

Jane felt like falling to the floor and drumming her heels on the black-and-white tiles. "I'm trapped, Alicia. If I stay it's inevitable we're going to end up sleeping together. It would put both of us in a difficult situation. If I leave, that won't happen." She smiled weakly. "Long-range planning. One of my strengths."

Her friend rolled her gaze. "Running from intimacy. One of your weaknesses."

Jane started chopping some fresh asparagus with noisy brutality.

Alicia finally stopped her with a hand on her arm.

"What if this is the real thing, honey? That doesn't come along every day. What about Spencer?"

A deep shiver trembled deep inside Jane. "Until the Marsden Holt account is awarded, I'll just keep avoiding him as much as possible."

"You're running away."

Jane didn't answer because she had an uncomfortable feeling that Alicia was right. But if she stayed at Datatracker and let the inevitable happen with Spencer, she'd have to explain to him and everyone she worked with that she'd lied to them about her marital status. They'd think she was nuts. He'd think she was nuts.

And she'd have to agree.

SPENCER LOGGED into his personal notebook and checked who he was seeing tonight. There was only one woman he wanted to see. The feel of her skin seemed imprinted on his palm. That and the memory of how her mouth had drawn him closer had him feeling stirred and restless.

Jane should be with him, not with a man who didn't appreciate her and ogled her best friend under her nose. He wanted to kick something. Instead he forced himself to focus on his date.

Simone. He quickly reviewed the details he'd stored about her.

She was a flight attendant, originally from Montreal. She was brunette, if he remembered correctly, and had an appealing French accent. He was pretty sure she also had a boyfriend in every terminal.

Not a gal with commitment on her mind, which was why he'd kept up with her. His cryptic notes informed him that she'd taken ballet in high school. Right. That's why he'd booked ballet tickets and dinner at a quiet French restaurant. He needed to get over his obsession with Jane. There was no way, after the little almost-incident in the parking lot that she didn't know how he felt. But while he was single, and able to pursue any relationship he wanted, she wasn't. There wasn't a damn thing he could do except try a little harder to be a gentleman.

A night out with free-spirited, sexy Simone was the first step in getting over Jane.

About halfway through dinner he wondered why he'd forgotten to log that irritating giggle. And had Simone smoked Gitaines when he'd dated her last?

By the time desert arrived he found himself thinking how much he liked Jane's laugh. It was soft and low. Ladylike. Maybe they taught them how to laugh at finishing school, but Jane's had a husky thread running through it. Just a whisper, but it caught him every time. Finishing school never taught her that.

Simone brayed again. Thank God they were seeing *Swan Lake*. He couldn't have taken anything comical.

After standing outside during intermission so Simone could smoke, and risking instant lung cancer from being squeezed in with a pack of nicotine addicts, Spencer made a mental note to delete Simone from his notebook.

He drove her back to her apartment, where she invited him up. He excused himself, and caught her glance of surprise. This wasn't the way their evenings usually ended, but she gave a Gallic shrug and leaned toward him for a good-night kiss. Since the idea of kissing her was about as appealing as licking a dirty ashtray, he coughed politely. "Think I'm coming down with a cold," he said and stuck out his hand, which she reluctantly shook.

Well, step one in Operation Get-Over-Jane had been a total and complete flop, he decided as he drove home, certain the smell of cigarette smoke still clung to the upholstery.

He only hoped he'd have better luck with the next couple of dates.

8

If Jane had been avoiding him before, she'd now become invisible.

Spencer checked the lot every morning for her car. And every morning he was in before her.

It was childish and mean-spirited of him, but the fact that she was going to such trouble to avoid him gave him a perverse satisfaction. It meant she was affected by him. It had to.

He cursed himself for acting like an adolescent even as he made excuses to visit the sales offices. Sometimes he glimpsed only the golden top of her head bent over her desk. Or he hovered in the corridor just to listen to the sound of her voice on the phone.

One day, he needed to go to Accounting and decided it was just as quick to get there through the sales department—if he sprinted.

He slowed as he passed the open door of Jane's office and heard a most unladylike curse.

Intrigued, he poked his head through the door and found her hammering keys and swearing at her computer. A navy suit jacket hung over the back of her chair and he could see the sheen of silk in her blouse as her arms bounced up and down.

A particularly ripe curse made him chuckle. "Don't tell me they taught you that in finishing school."

Her hand flew up to her mouth guiltily as she swung to face him. "Oh, Spencer. I didn't think anyone could hear me." Maybe the slight flush that rose in her cheeks and the hitch in her breath were a result of embarrassment at being caught cursing, but he preferred to think it was seeing him that had her acting that way. "I'm just so mad. I've lost part of the new proposal I'm working on for Marsden Holt."

He forgot about her unladylike swearing. This was the first he'd heard about any movement on the Marsden Holt deal. "New proposal?"

She dropped her gaze and fiddled with her ring. "I was going to tell you about it in tomorrow's sales meeting. The client requested some new information and some system modifications. I wanted to have a draft ready for you tomorrow."

Two weeks ago she would have come into his office the minute she heard from them. Two weeks ago, she wouldn't have handed him the proposal in a crowded meeting room. But then two weeks ago he hadn't almost kissed her.

He looked at her face but she wouldn't meet his eyes.

He could berate her for failing to keep him informed on developments on an account he was involved in. He could haul her on the carpet for... Well, the things he could haul her on the carpet for were X-rated.

He could also be a decent guy and help her out of a jam. He didn't seem to know squat about women, but computers he understood.

"What's the problem?" He gestured to the computer, which sat innocently enough on her desk, its cursor blinking quietly.

"It crashed while I was working. When I rebooted it the new material was gone."

"Show me."

Jane swiveled her chair back around and went through the motions of retrieving the file. As the words came up on her screen she shook her head. "It's still the old file."

Spencer leaned over her. "May I?" His hand hovered over the computer's mouse.

"Yes, of course." Jane moved her hand away in a quick, nervous gesture. The plastic was still warm from her hand when he touched it.

She tried to rise but he put his other hand on her shoulder. "Watch and learn," he commanded. He felt the rigid tension in her shoulder as she sat back down. He left his hand there for only a moment—long enough to feel the warmth from her skin heating the silk. He removed his hand and rested it on the desktop instead.

He could do this stuff with his eyes closed. He talked to the computer in its own language—let it know what he wanted, helped it find the new version. And while he did that he felt Jane's heat scorching him through her blouse. Her hair stirred every time he breathed and he caught the scent of almonds.

Their heads were so close that if she turned his way their lips would meet. Her chest was rising and falling more rapidly than normal and as much as he told himself not to, he couldn't stop his eyes from tracing the shape of her breasts through the silk and lace.

She never moved. She kept her head facing the screen, but her body let him know that his nearness was getting to her. Her nipples blossomed before his eyes and he felt an answering hardening in his own body.

He wondered if the skin of her neck was as silky to the touch as it looked. He imagined her glorious hair unbound and spilling free while he made love to her.

Blinking back the images before his brain crashed worse than this computer, he explained what he was doing to retrieve her document.

In an ego-boostingly short time, he had the file back.

"There. Is that the right version?" His voice came out hoarsely.

"Yes. Thanks a lot." Jane didn't even turn her head to look at him. She seemed to know that if she turned and met his eyes he'd throw himself to his knees before her. And she was too smart to let that happen.

And too married.

SPENCER FORGOT all about his errand to Accounting. He left Jane and headed right past his office door and past Yumi's desk. "I'm going out for a while. I'll call in later."

He ignored her startled protest and kept walking, out into the hallway, down the elevator and out onto the street.

The truth was tough to accept. He was falling in love with a married woman. She was trying to avoid him, and he, Saint Spencer, was doing his best to make that impossible.

One sign, one positive move on her part in the office and he would have lost control. If she'd so much as touched him, or looked at him a certain way he would have moved forward—taken her mouth and to hell with the consequences. He would have demanded that she face up to the growing attraction between them.

He wanted Jane as he'd never wanted anything in his life. The fact that she was married hurt. It hurt like hell. But it didn't stop him from wanting her. He raised his hands to his face and noticed they were shaking. He felt sick inside. He was no better than Karen.

He'd spent a long time hating his ex-wife, blaming her for the wreck of their marriage—for betraying him with another man and then leaving him.

He remembered one of their last conversations before she moved out. Well, he hadn't been conversing really, more like ranting at Karen while she cried. He'd thrown the emotional book at her. Finally she rose, wiped streaming eyes and said, "Why don't you get some counseling? Maybe someone else could help you see there's more than one side to this story."

Karen would be happy. Finally he was seeing the other side of the story. In fact, he was acting it out.

When he was married to Karen he'd had another love. It had drawn him irresistibly, held him in thrall when he should have been home with his wife. His true love's name was Datatracker.

It was as though a blindfold had been removed. When he looked at his marriage now, he could see that he hadn't been much of a husband. He and Karen had married young. He couldn't even remember why, now that he looked back. But he hadn't made her happy.

And with a gasp of shock he realized that she hadn't made him happy, either.

Her lover and current husband Jim made her happy.

Just as Jane made him happy.

He walked blindly. It was one of those damp, drizzly days on which only the wusses and tourists bothered with umbrellas. Wetness collected on his skin and hair and beaded his sweater, but he didn't care. He wanted misery. The more the better.

Assuming Jane was as attracted as he was, and it was a big, egotistical assumption on his part, could he ask her to leave her marriage for him?

He pulled up short. No. He couldn't.

He walked into a Starbucks, ordered a coffee to warm him and decided he needed to explore other options. He hadn't given his plan to date other women enough of a chance. Simone had been a disaster, but maybe Tara, a model he'd met somewhere, would provide more of a distraction from his growing obsession with Jane....

9

TEN MINUTES into the date with Tara later that same night, Spencer knew he'd made another mistake. He was really going to have to streamline that date database, he thought. They started out at a trendy bar where he ordered a pepper martini, intrigued by the name. Tara ordered a Perrier, which she sipped cautiously.

"You don't drink?" he asked. He wished he'd remembered that detail. If he had he would have taken her to a juice bar or something. He had to start paying more attention to his dates' preferences if he wanted to find a woman with whom he could get serious.

The realization that he was ready to get serious again surprised him, but he realized it was true. Somewhere along the line he'd stopped resenting Karen and accepted that they'd simply married too young and mistaken lust for love. It had been a mistake but at least they hadn't had children to suffer for their error. He still wished they'd parted before Jim had come on the scene, but he was a little older and a lot more philosophical now.

Tara shook her teased, dyed mane. "I have to count every calorie."

She was wearing a tiny dress that showed off her even tinier body. The woman was all bones and hollows. She looked as if she'd crumble to dust if he touched her—all but the big breasts that looked absurd on her skeletal frame.

Now he was no expert, but he didn't think any woman that thin could grow breasts that large. When she moved, they didn't. In fact, they looked like meringues, but, of course, they couldn't be since she'd never let so much sugar get near her model-thin body.

Jane had real breasts. They were much smaller than Tara's but they were soft and natural. He'd snuck a peek when he was bending over her at the computer. Yes, they were the perfect size.

Tara looked as though she'd fall on her face when she stood just from weight imbalance. Funny how he'd never noticed that before.

He downed his drink in record time—even though he had discovered an aversion to pepper martinis—to get on to dinner so he could get home sooner. "I booked Il Paradiso for dinner. Is that okay?"

"Sure." She nodded enthusiastically. "It's a very see-and-be-seen place. My friend saw Gwyneth Paltrow there. I'll spend an extra hour at the gym tomorrow to make up for the extra calories, that's all."

He didn't think the evening could deteriorate any further. Not until they were seated at the restaurant. He was sipping his second martini—Tara had an untouched Perrier in front of her—while she deconstructed the menu. The woman had a fat calculator built into her brain.

He didn't know why it irritated him so much. A low-fat diet was certainly healthy. That was it, he thought.

She probably couldn't care less about health. The woman was simply obsessed with her looks.

She ordered organic spinach salad with no dressing, just a little vinegar on the side and a plate of raw carrots. The waiter didn't seem fazed, not even when she asked if any of the pastas were macrobiotic.

"I'm sorry, no."

"That's okay." She fished in her purse and pulled out a plastic bag with a couple of crumbly beige disks inside. "I brought my own macrobiotic brown rice cakes. That's what Liz Hurley does. She takes them everywhere."

Spence took one look at the dull beige macrobiotic whatevers and perversely chose what looked like the richest, fattest, most cholesterol-laden items he could find on the menu. "Think I'll have the *coquilles Saint Jacques* to start," he told the waiter, "and then the steak and lobster." Tara's shocked gasp made him add, "With extra butter."

He closed his menu and glanced casually around the restaurant, wondering if anyone else was as miserable as he.

A few tables away sat a couple looking so cozily in love they caught his attention.

The man was in the act of leaning over to give his dining companion a full-lipped kiss. The gesture struck Spencer as over-the-top in a restaurant, but whatever. At least they were having more fun at their table than he was at his.

His gaze had started to move on when the lip-lock broke up and with a start he recognized the male diner as Chuck.

Spence's heart thudded in his chest and he felt his fists clench. That wasn't Jane Chuck had been smooching so enthusiastically he didn't notice his tie trailing in his salad. Spence could only see her back, but the woman's hair wasn't blond and smooth, but black and kinky.

His gaze narrowed, Spencer watched Chuck straighten his glasses and reach into his pocket to pull out a squat velvet ring box.

His initial impulse, to go pound Chuck into steak tartare for having cheated on Jane—and with her best friend—gave way to intrigue as the woman opened the jewelry box and uttered a shriek.

He watched as Chuck leaned over and removed a ring from the box. Alicia presented her left hand, while wiping a tear away with her right, and Chuck slipped the ring onto her wedding-ring finger. On top of two other rings. She turned the ring around and around, and Spence caught the flash of diamonds. What did they call those things?

Eternity rings.

The truth struck him and he couldn't believe he hadn't figured it out earlier. Chuck wasn't married to Jane, he was married to Jane's best friend, Alicia. And happily—presumably for eternity.

They were so wrapped up in each other, giggling and holding hands and, yes, smooching again, that he felt safe staring at them.

SPENCER HAD NEVER BEEN happier to witness another couple's marital bliss. Especially given the evidence before his eyes that Jane wasn't half of that happy couple.

He began to smile. If she wasn't married to Chuck, it seemed logical to assume she wasn't married at all.

Spencer felt as though a fist that had been squeezing his vital organs had opened its grip. The awful pressure in his chest eased instantly.

Jane wasn't married.

His attraction to her wasn't adulterous.

He started to rise, thinking he'd go over to Chuck and Alicia's table and have a little fun at their expense, but only an instant's thought was necessary to banish that idea.

No. If she knew he knew, Alicia would be on her cell phone warning Jane that the jig was up before the main course was served.

For the moment, he'd keep this novel and rather bizarre news to himself.

One thing was certain. Chuck and Alicia might have eyes only for each other, but they were bound to glance around eventually. Every second he remained here, he was in danger of being seen by the anniversary couple. And that would definitely not suit him.

He gulped the rest of his martini, thinking he had to bolt and do it fast.

"Hello-o," Tara intruded on his thoughts in a petulant tone.

"I'm sorry, Tara. I just remembered something really important I forgot to do."

Her penciled eyebrows rose. "Can't it wait until after dinner?"

"No. I'm sorry. I feel like a jerk, but it's an urgent

business matter." He realized he was acting like a heel, and tried to think of a way to make it up to his date. "Have you got a friend who could join you for dinner? On me? I'll leave an imprint of my credit card on my way out. Have champagne, dessert, whatever you want."

"But whoever I invite will have to eat all that fat you ordered," Tara pointed out. He thought she was going to refuse, but suddenly her eyes gleamed. She shrugged and dug in her bag with a red-tipped hand for her phone.

"Larisa, sweetie, how'd you like to have dinner at Il Paradiso...?" A moment later she nodded and waved him on his way.

He left her chattering to her friend and gazing around for famous people. He'd be willing to bet that Larisa sweetie was even skinnier than Tara.

Luckily, Alicia and Chuck were still so engrossed in each other they didn't have any attention to spare for other diners. Still, he eased out of Il Paradiso as quickly and quietly as he could. He didn't want any of the actors in Jane's marriage farce knowing he'd caught on— not until he was good and ready to stage his own scene.

He wobbled a bit when he hit the sidewalk, realizing he was slightly buzzed from two martinis on an empty stomach. He should get something to eat, he thought. He should go home. But he didn't want to eat. He didn't want to go home.

He called a cab and then tried to decide where he wanted to go. It didn't take him more than a nano-second.

With this new and incredible development, he could only think of Jane. He had to see her. Would he feel differently when he saw her, now that he knew she was a single woman?

He'd never been to her apartment, but he'd peeked at her personnel file. He knew where she lived. He gave her address to the driver and settled back on the cracked vinyl seat of the cab, wondering how he was going to play this.

As the yellow cab cruised the rain-slicked streets, relief flooded through him. She was single. He was single. The world suddenly seemed like a happier place.

Her behavior struck him as more than a little odd, though. Why would a woman pretend to be married? It was the strangest damn thing he'd ever heard. He should check with his old buddy at Graham's and see if Jane had pretended to be married there.

Sucking in a breath caused him almost to gag on the smell of pine air freshener.

He had only the haziest idea what he'd say when he got to her door, but he knew he had to see her tonight. He paid off the cab and heard it slide away through the quiet street until he was alone in front of her building.

The barrier that she'd erected between them didn't exist. That meant Saint Spencer could have the night off. He strode to the entry, found her apartment number and buzzed.

It hadn't occurred to him she might not be home, but of course, she could be anywhere, and he could be stuck out here like a jackass in the rain, with no wheels.

But she was home. Her voice sounded soft and husky even through the distortion of the intercom.

"Jane. It's Spencer. I need to talk to you."

There was a long pause, and for a second he thought she might refuse. "It's about business," he shouted at the intercom.

"All right," she said. "Come up." She sounded wary. Smart lady.

She opened the door and her beauty struck him afresh, even stronger now that he didn't have to deny his attraction.

"Spencer, what a surprise." Her voice didn't sound calm or serene, it sounded nervous, edgy.

Now that he was here, he had no idea what to say. He stood there for a moment feeling absolutely foolish. Then inspiration struck. For the way she'd made him suffer, perhaps a little payback was in order. "Sorry to call unannounced. I was just passing and I wanted to talk to Chuck about something."

She stared at him as though he'd lost his mind. "You want to talk to Chuck? What about? I thought you said it was business."

Right. He and old Chuck hadn't exactly bonded on the two occasions when they'd met. Trying to say something that made sense took more than the usual effort. For that he blamed the woman in front of him. She caused such a rush of lust to slam through him that it short-circuited his brain.

"Race cars," he managed at last.

"Race cars?"

"Yes. You mentioned they're one of his hobbies. In the Chicago airport. Remember?"

"Ye-es. I remember." She looked as though she wished she didn't.

"Well, I'm thinking about getting some tickets to the Molson Indy." *Business, business. What did this have to do with business?* "I'm thinking about giving out tickets to some of our clients. I was going to ask him about it." Not bad, he thought, for something off the top of his head.

She blushed. A guilty blush or a happy-to-see-him blush? He wished he knew. "Um, Chuck's not here right now."

No, and Spencer could tell her exactly where her precious husband was. Instead, he tried to look disappointed. "Will he be long? Maybe I could wait for him."

She pushed at her hair. He noticed the way the light caught it and turned it to spun gold. He wanted to free it from the barrette she was wearing and run his fingers through the soft strands. "Actually, he's out of town."

"I love the way you say 'actually.' So clipped and upper-class." He leaned against the doorjamb enjoying the view.

A furrow formed between her brows. He wanted to kiss it away.

"Have you been drinking, Spencer?"

He shrugged. "Couple of martinis."

Her eyes widened. "You weren't driving were you?"

He also loved the way she sounded all motherly, as though she was worried about him. He smiled, deep into her eyes. "I caught a cab."

"You had a couple of martinis and took a cab to my house to talk to Chuck about race cars?"

"No. I was passing by in the cab. Suddenly thought about the Indy. Decided to come and see y—Chuck."

Reluctantly she backed up into her apartment. "You'd better come in and have some coffee. Then we'll call you another cab."

He wandered down the hall behind her enjoying the way she filled out a pair of jeans.

"Have a seat." She gestured to a chintz-covered floral sofa. He sank gratefully into it while she moved into the kitchenette and bustled around efficiently.

Even her apartment smelled good. He noticed bowls of potpourri on an antique writing desk and atop a well-stocked bookcase. He liked her stuff, a mixture of quality antiques and modern pieces. Stylish but comfortable.

And feminine. He liked that best of all.

There were no signs of a man living here that he could see. Of course, the living room wasn't going to give away a lot of secrets. He needed to do some more investigating before giving into his conclusion that she was, in fact, single.

"May I use your washroom?" He asked.

"Of course, down the hall to the right."

It was the guest bathroom, he realized once he was inside. Nicely decorated in mocha tones, but impersonal. He sneaked a peek in the medicine cabinet and only found little bottles of shampoo, some guest soap and an unopened toothbrush. Spencer the supersleuth had discovered that she was a thoughtful hostess, but he'd found out nothing new about Jane's love life.

On his way back to the living room, he noticed a door ajar. It had to be her bedroom. Feeling like a Peeping Tom, he gave the door a little nudge with his foot and peered inside.

Everything looked elegant and neat, kind of like Jane herself. The room was done in soft green and cream. Nice big bed, he noted. No sign of a man living there, but no sign there wasn't one, either.

The trouble with tidy people was that they were harder to figure out. They didn't leave clues all over the floor with the dirty laundry—as he did.

Still, all that chintz in the living room wasn't exactly macho, he mused as he continued on to the living room. And those cushions had frills on them. What self-respecting man—even one like Chuck—was going to sit on a floral sofa with a frilled cushion at his back? He sighed and sat down on it when he reached it. Him for one, especially if he could tip Jane back on those frills and kiss her senseless. Carry her to the big bed and make love to her until she was panting, on the edge of ecstasy....

"I'm almost there," Jane's voice called. He thought it was part of his fantasy until he realized it was her real voice coming from the kitchen. And she didn't mean what he wanted her to mean.

He'd better get himself under control, and fast. There were a few photographs in frames on the mantel over the gas fireplace. He got up to peruse them. He saw two stiff-looking dignified types he guessed were her parents, and a group of skiers posed at the bottom of a steep ski run laughing into the camera. He spotted Jane right away in a sky-blue ski suit.

The third photo showed Chuck flanked by Jane and Alicia. He had an arm around each of them and was smiling broadly. It was a wedding picture, but Jane wasn't the one wearing the wedding dress. Alicia was. Jane, gorgeous in a pale-green silk dress, was clearly the bridesmaid. "And that one's worth a thousand words," Spencer murmured to himself.

The smell of freshly brewed coffee made him turn toward the kitchen. She had stools that pulled up to a granite breakfast bar. He took off his suit jacket and tossed it over the back of the couch before heading to the adjacent kitchenette. He pulled up a kitchen stool so he could watch Jane in the kitchen.

She handed him a small tray with a blue china mug full of steaming coffee, and matching cream and sugar dispensers. He sipped his coffee slowly, enjoying watching her bustle around in her kitchen.

She didn't return his gaze. She opened the fridge and asked over her shoulder, "Did you have any dinner?"

"Couple of olives. No—" he thought back to the martini bar "—one of them might have been a peppercorn."

Her fridge was stocked with real food. He noticed butter, cheese, vegetables, fruit. Even a box of chocolates. Not a low-fat label in sight. He liked Jane more each time he saw her.

She pulled out butter, eggs, cheese and mushrooms. "How does an omelet sound?"

"Made with your own hands it sounds sensational."

He let his gaze travel down her slim form, liking the fact that her soft, womanly body featured not a scrap of silicone. "You don't work out obsessively, do you?"

She shot him an amused look and shook her head. "I

belong to a fitness center. Mostly I swim. Why, do I look like I need to work out?"

"Jane, one of the things I like best about you is that you neither need nor want a model-skinny body. You're beautiful just the way you are."

"Drink your coffee." She sounded as if she was laughing at him, but it was hard to tell because she was fiddling at the stove and still wouldn't look at him.

She put one large omelet on a plate in front of him, then went back to more kitchen busywork.

This wouldn't do. He didn't want to feel as though he was in a restaurant. He wanted to feel as if he were having dinner with Jane. "You're not having one?"

She shook her head. "I ate earlier."

"I may not have gone to finishing school, but I can't sit here and eat while you work in the kitchen." He patted the seat beside him. "Come join me."

Reluctantly she complied, filling a mug and sitting with it, not in the seat he'd indicated, but one over. That left a seat between them, concrete proof that she didn't dare sit too close to him.

He eyed the empty stool and then her, giving her a grin that let her know he knew she was chicken. She brought her hand to her throat as though checking for buttons, and fiddled with the V-neck of her sweater.

He didn't think anything on the menu of a fancy restaurant could beat the flavor of the steaming omelet. The mushrooms were juicier, the cheese sharper, the eggs more buttery, the toast crunchier than any he'd ever tasted. "This is fantastic," he raved between mouthfuls.

He felt happier than he had in days, really being

with her instead of sneaking around snatching glimpses and feeling guilty. His attraction was honest, acceptable. He only had to get her admitting to her own attraction and her single state, and they'd soon be having the passionate relationship he'd been dreaming about.

He polished off the omelet, then insisted on helping her with the dishes, which confined them together in the small galley kitchen. Despite her protests, he squeezed in beside her to dry the dishes. Their arms inadvertently touched as they worked side by side, and each time it happened he felt a thrill course through his body.

He glanced at Jane and noticed her color was up. He didn't think the blush was from the steam coming off the suds, though she kept herself bent over the sink as though she'd be punished if she lifted her head.

"Well..." she began briskly, drying her hands on a tea towel.

"How about a game of Scrabble?" he interrupted. He was grasping at straws, but he didn't want to hear her tell him it was time to leave.

"Scrabble?" She turned her glorious gaze on him and he saw a mixture of merriment and distrust.

He shrugged. "Monopoly, Pictionary, strip poker? I'm not fussy."

She laughed. That thread of whiskey running through the cool sound was intoxicating. "I've never been much of a poker player."

"Well, gentleman that I am, I'll give myself a handicap." He looked her up and down, and this time the rosy blush had nothing to do with the kitchen sink. "I figure you're wearing—oh—about six items including the socks. Am I right?"

She pursed her lips, but her eyes were still dancing. He didn't know whether she was going to smack him or play along. He held his breath.

"You're close." She gestured to her feet beneath the jeans and wiggled her toes. "Those aren't socks. They're tights. One item."

"All right. Five items. And I'm wearing...let's see...tie, shirt, pants, briefs, two socks, two shoes. That's eight. I'll strip down to two things. Just to even the playing field."

Her pursed lips were losing the battle, he noticed. She was struggling against another smile. "Which two things?"

He grinned. "My socks, of course."

The air was fraught with the kind of tension only a kiss could break. Spencer had a feeling that kissing those soft, slightly parted lips would expedite his departure, but it might also expedite getting the truth out of her about her marital status. Besides, he had to touch her in some way.

Swiftly, he reached behind her head and released the silver hair clip. She started as her hair danced out of its bondage and waved softly round her shoulders.

He held the clasp up. "That's your handicap. Can't have you too far ahead of me."

She crossed her arms, looking both excited and offended at the same time. "Really, Spencer."

"Come on," he teased. "Playing strip poker with me is probably a lot more fun than whatever you were doing when I got here."

A gleam of mischief sparked in her eyes. "That depends on how much fun you think it would be to bag Marsden Holt."

"A beauty and a workaholic. Damn, I wish you weren't married."

He'd been teasing, but the minute the words were out of his mouth he wanted to swallow them. Jane's hand flew to her mouth as her cheeks flooded with color. She looked at the ring on her hand as if she'd never seen it before. "That's right! Whatever was I thinking?"

Frankly, he was wondering the same thing, but until she told him that she'd been posing as a married woman, and why, he'd have to respect the barrier she'd put between them. Even if it was only a make-believe husband and a dime-store ring.

He grabbed his suit jacket off the back of the chair and slipped it on. "I should be going, anyway. Thanks for dinner, Jane."

"I'll call you a cab."

"No. I need the air. I'll walk. And don't work any more tonight. That's an order."

"But the sales meeting's tomorrow. I wanted to have the new proposal finished."

"Relax. Whenever you finish it you can drop it by Yumi's desk. You don't even have to see the big bad wolf."

"I don't..."

He watched color invade her cheeks once again as he paused at the door. "Avoid me? You do. And your instincts are right on."

"They are?" Her voice sounded almost yearning, as though she wanted him to prove her wrong.

"Oh, yes." Unable to stop himself, he moved closer, so close they were almost touching. "You know what I'd do right now if you weren't a married woman don't you?"

"No," she said softly, provocatively. "What?"

His hands were instantly cupping her face, soft silky hair trailing over them.

He kissed her. Not hard and not deep, but enough to let the woman know—if she could possibly be in any doubt—that he was crazy about her.

She made a soft sound against his lips. Not a sigh. Not a moan. More of a muffled, "Yes."

He pulled away before the touch and smell and taste of her had him telling her he knew she was single, and forcing her to face this thing between them.

"This," he said softly, and pulled away.

Her eyes were large and darkly purple and she looked more than a little stunned.

He'd given her something to think about all right. He touched her cheek. "'Night."

10

THE DOOR closed behind Spencer and Jane swiftly locked and chained it, then turned and leaned against the door still feeling the imprint of his lips on hers.

What had she been thinking? Never mind doing. Flirting with the man, kissing him.

Oh, Lord help her, she'd enjoyed having him in her home, loved cooking for him, and she didn't even want to contemplate what that semi-chaste kiss had done to her system. Spence must have noticed her response though. Which was bad.

Worse, he had penetrated her home. And for a while tonight she had drifted into the fantasy that he was hers. He looked oddly at home in the feminine apartment. Maybe because he was so very masculine, he seemed to balance the chintz and flowers.

One thing was for sure, he was getting too close for comfort. He certainly hadn't been drunk, but Jane didn't think a completely sober Spencer would have showed up at her apartment unannounced. She hoped the two martinis had dulled his senses enough that he hadn't noticed there wasn't a trace of any husband in her apartment.

She'd better get into high gear and land that Marsden Holt account so she could leave with a clean conscience and her head held high. Then, when he wasn't her boss any longer, she'd be free to call him and see whether there was something real between them.

Ignoring Spencer's direct order, she spent several hours in the spare bedroom cum office at her computer, wrestling with the new proposal.

It was late when she finally called it a night. As she undressed, she counted each piece of clothing she removed. His count had been slightly off. Sweater...one, jeans...two, tights...three, panties...four. She hadn't told Spencer she wasn't wearing a bra.

She imagined playing strip poker with him as she slipped into a cotton nightgown and washed and brushed her teeth. As she climbed into bed, her imagination conjured him in nothing but his socks.

It was a long time before she slept.

SPENCER WOKE early. At first he felt as though he'd invented a new system. Something truly incredible must have happened to have him waking like a kid on his birthday, he thought.

Then he remembered and a slow smile split his face. He thumped the pillow and rolled to his back, clasping his hands behind his head to consider the events of the last night.

There was the ta-da! moment when he'd watched Chuck put an eternity ring on Jane's best friend's finger and the slightly inebriated visit he'd paid Jane. He cringed slightly when he thought about how he'd dropped in uninvited, but a little humiliation was well worth the ultimate discovery that there was no man living at her address.

Why a grown woman would pretend to be married

stumped him. He sighed. Jane seemed sane and intelligent. He drummed his knuckles against his pine headboard while he tried to puzzle it out.

The clock informed him it was six-fifteen. By the time he'd had a quick shower and was sipping the first java of the day, it was six-thirty and he knew his sister-in-law would be up. If anyone could help him solve this puzzle, it was Chelsea.

He punched one on his speed-dial. She answered on the second ring.

"How's it going?" he said brightly.

There was a tiny pause. "Oh. I thought that might be your brother calling."

He heard the disappointment in her tone and immediately wished it were his brother who'd phoned her. "Haven't talked to him for a while, huh? Me neither. No e-mails either. He's probably off in a sandbox somewhere digging up bones."

"Yes. I suppose. And you would be calling me at the crack of dawn because?"

"What's the point of having a psychologist in the family if you can't call her up for free counseling at an ungodly hour?"

"Nothing in this life is free, bro. You want advice for the lovelorn, I take it?"

He winced. How obvious he must have appeared that day they'd gone inline skating. He prayed it was only because she was a trained observer of human nature that she'd noticed his infatuation with Jane. "Yes. I want to talk to you about something."

"It will cost you breakfast."

NO POSTAGE
NECESSARY
IF MAILED
IN THE
UNITED STATES

BUSINESS REPLY MAIL

FIRST-CLASS MAIL   PERMIT NO. 717-003   BUFFALO, NY

POSTAGE WILL BE PAID BY ADDRESSEE

HARLEQUIN READER SERVICE
3010 WALDEN AVE
PO BOX 1867
BUFFALO NY 14240-9952

If offer card is missing write to: Harlequin Reader Service, 3010 Walden Ave., P.O. Box 1867, Buffalo NY 14240-1867

Get FREE BOOKS and a FREE GIFT when you play the...

LAS VEGAS
GAME

7

Just scratch off the gold box with a coin. Then check below to see the gifts you get! →

YES! I have scratched off the gold Box. Please send me my 2 FREE BOOKS and gift for which I qualify. I understand that I am under no obligation to purchase any books as explained on the back of this card.

342 HDL DUYP   **142 HDL DUY5**

FIRST NAME	LAST NAME

ADDRESS

APT.#	CITY

STATE/PROV.   ZIP/POSTAL CODE   (H-T-03/03)

7	7	7	Worth TWO FREE BOOKS plus a BONUS Mystery Gift!
🍒	🍒	🍒	Worth TWO FREE BOOKS!
🔔	🔔	♣	TRY AGAIN!

Visit us online at www.eHarlequin.com

Offer limited to one per household and not valid to current Harlequin Temptation® subscribers. All orders subject to approval.

"Done."

They met at a coffee shop they both liked with a view of Jericho Beach. By seven they'd been served, which left them with a half hour to talk.

Chelsea dug into her yogurt-and-fruit plate and he bit into his first slice of toast.

She glanced at him in surprise. "You always have the bacon and sausage. What's with the omelet?"

"I felt like a change." He tried to shrug casually. The truth was, he hadn't realized what he was ordering. The omelet was a link to the one Jane had cooked him the night before. How pathetic was that?

"So. What's up?"

"Jane's not married." He hadn't meant to blurt it out like that, but hell, he and Chelsea both had to get to work and he didn't have a lot of time to beat around the bush.

Her face remained impassive as she chose a cantaloupe ball and calmly ate it. "No one can get divorced instantly in this country, Spence. Do you mean she's separated? That can be—"

"No. I'm telling you, Jane's not married to Chuck. I don't think she's ever been married."

Chelsea blinked, chewed slowly and swallowed. "I think you're going to have to explain exactly what you're talking about."

So he did, giving Chelsea a full rundown of his enlightening evening at Il Paradiso and taking her right up to the good-night kiss.

When he was finished the recital, Chelsea said, "Well, that is unusual."

"Unusual? It's pretty damned insane if you ask me, which is why I immediately thought of you."

His breakfast companion choked. "Thank you."

He grinned across the table at her. "You know what I mean. What I want to know is, why would a woman do that?"

Once again, Chelsea took her time answering. It took two pineapple cubes and a spoonful of yogurt and granola before he got his answer.

"Protection. That would be my best guess. Figure it out, Spencer. You told me she lost her last job because some creep hit on her and in retaliating she ended up fired, right. I imagine she receives unwelcome advances all the time. She's single and beautiful, so men take that to mean she's available."

"Not all men," he insisted.

Chelsea sent him a level look. "Some men. A 'husband' is the easiest way out of a sticky situation for a woman who travels a lot."

It irritated him to hear the old "men are pigs" argument coming from his own sister-in-law. "Whatever happened to 'No thanks?'"

"Come on, Spencer. Put yourself in her situation. Maybe she's selling a system, and maybe the guy with the buying power takes it into his head to get a crush on her."

"What you're talking about is—"

"Reality, sweet cheeks. I'm not saying it happens all the time. But 'Sorry, I'm married,' is a lot easier for a man to take than 'Sorry, I'm not interested.'" She smiled a little crookedly. "I know it was one benefit of marriage I was happy to acquire, and I'm not nearly as beautiful as Jane."

"You're saying this insane masquerade has your approval?" He was torn between being so delighted he wanted to run after Jane and kiss her senseless, to being so frustrated he wanted to kick something.

"Of course it doesn't have my approval. I'm merely trying to explain to you how Jane may have rationalized her decision to pose as a married woman. If that's what she's doing. Which we don't know for certain."

"Chelsea, I saw Chuck in the restaurant. He was nuzzling Jane's best friend and sticking an eternity ring on her finger. And it doesn't take a PhD in psychology to figure out that Jane and Chuck have absolutely nothing in common. You saw them in the park that day. It was obvious something funny was going on. Remember when Jane and her friend were kicking the poor guy black and blue? I'm telling you, Jane and Chuck aren't married."

"There are a lot of marriages that make you wonder." She sighed. "Mine for one. That's all I'm saying. Don't get too excited until you know for sure."

"But I'm positive she's single. And I'm close to certain that she's attracted to me, too."

"If what you say is true, why hasn't she told you herself she's available?"

He swallowed a bite of omelet, thinking Jane's had been a lot tastier. He wondered when she'd be cooking him one for breakfast. He hoped it was soon. "So you don't think I should challenge her?"

"More than you already have by showing up at her

door uninvited, making suggestive comments and kissing her? No, Spence. I think you should continue with your subtle approach."

He forked up some hash browns and chewed without tasting. "Okay, maybe I was a little out of line last night. But I've never felt like this about anyone. Not even Karen."

Chelsea's face softened and she touched his hand with her own. "I know. Give Jane some time. When she's ready, she'll tell you the truth."

He sighed, sipping more coffee. Chelsea was right. If Jane wanted to explore the chemistry that was sizzling between them it was up to her to tell him the truth.

"Okay. So—" he glanced at his watch "—the session's not over yet. There are still a few minutes remaining. Why don't you tell me what's going on with you and my brother."

"He's in Africa, I'm in Canada. What could possibly be going on?"

"You're pissed with him. I'm not stupid. What gives?"

She traced a pattern into her yogurt. "I want to have a baby."

Immediately he thought about being an uncle and the idea filled him with glee. "That's great, Chels! I'll be a terrific uncle. I can teach the little tyke about electronics, buy him his first computer game, help him navigate the Internet—"

"Well, first, the little tyke may be a she, and then there's the problem of Bill and me being on the same continent long enough to conceive, and the little tyke having a father who doesn't spend half his life close to war zones or simply being unavailable."

Spence felt his brows crease. "My brother was smart enough to marry you, Chelsea. He's got to be smart enough to work out a compromise."

She snorted. "I asked him to give up field work so we could have a child." She dropped her spoon so suddenly, yogurt splashed.

"And what did he say?" Spence knew his brother. Asking him to give up his field work would be like someone asking Spencer to give up his computer.

"He said we'll talk about it when he gets home. In that tone he uses when he means no."

"You know, kid, I'm no psychologist like you are, but have you done any compromising yourself? Put yourself in Bill's shoes. What if he asked you to give up counseling work outside of teaching? You love that as much as he loves digging for old bones."

"I might have known you'd side with your brother," she said, rising.

"I'm not siding with him." He tossed down some bills and followed her out of the café. "I love you both and I think you love each other enough to work this out." He hugged her and patted her back. "Don't screw up."

Chelsea laughed weakly. "Back at you."

He drove to work torn between worry about Bill and Chelsea's love life and filled with hope about his own. Although, until he could get Jane to admit they had a love life, his hands were effectively tied.

Or were they? He agreed with Chelsea that it was up

to Jane to own up to the truth, especially after her history with Johnson, but nobody said he had to sit back passively and wait.

In his non-expert opinion, the kiss last night had got her thinking. He chuckled as he parked in his space. Maybe the lady needed further encouragement.

He had a couple of ideas.

11

SPENCER BROKE OFF whistling to greet Yumi and grab one of her homemade granola muffins on his way past her desk, swapping it for the take-out latte he'd brought her. He had an identical cup in his other hand.

Yumi eyed him, then the cup, with suspicion. "What's in there? Happy juice?"

He merely winked and took a big bite of muffin. The happy juice wasn't in the take-out cup. It pumped through his system.

Once in his office, he flipped on his computer, put his jacket on the back of his chair and checked his e-mail. While he scanned his messages, he contemplated his own situation. He couldn't believe he'd actually fallen for Jane's con. He grinned to himself, reliving again that moment when the scales had fallen from his eyes.

Jane was single. And he was single. And the bubbling attraction between them was normal and healthy.

He rubbed his chin, not noticing that the tweed jacket he'd slung over the back of his chair had fallen to the floor.

She hadn't admitted her single state when he'd kissed her last night, so, obviously, he needed sneakier tactics. How to get to her?

How?

A slow smile crept up his face. His fingers made a sound like a firecracker as he snapped them in the quiet office.

He'd seen the jolt of surprise in her eyes when she'd spotted Chelsea at the company party. Surprise, and, unless he was delusional, a trace of jealousy. He'd seen it again when she'd literally bumped into him at the park the following day.

He knew how he'd felt when she'd described her hunk of a husband. Maybe it was time to parade a little more arm candy under her nose, just to give her a nudge.

But how was he going to let her know he was dating beautiful single women without sounding like a puffed-up braggart?

He frowned over that until the most brilliant idea of his life—if you didn't include the RDT-100—popped into his head.

If Jane could invent characters, so could he. He'd cancelled on bachelorette number three, but Jane didn't have to know that.

She was on the phone when he dropped by her office. When she saw him, she began to stutter. He watched with pleasure as her eyes widened, that wonderful bluey-purple of her irises darkening to indigo. He nodded and lounged in her doorway, content to wait until she was off the phone.

His scrutiny was bringing a slight blush to her cheeks. Or maybe that was the remembered kiss. He was remembering it, anyway. Couldn't help himself. She'd felt, tasted and sounded so good that he knew he'd have to bite his tongue to stop himself from challenging her about her lie.

"I'm sorry?" she said into the receiver and swiveled her chair slightly so she wasn't looking directly at him "Oh, no. The R-220 won't be in production until spring." She laughed. "I can ask."

She was trying to act normally, but he saw her hand creep up to her throat to check that all her buttons were fastened. He didn't need Chelsea whispering in his ear to figure out that the lady was checking her defenses. Good. He fully intended to breach them. Or better still, make them crumble beneath his sensual assault.

When she finished the call, he jumped right in to attack.

"I'm sorry I missed Chuck last night."

"Chuck? Oh, yes. I um...I shouldn't have..." Her hand now crept toward her far-too-kissable lips.

He didn't want to hear her say she shouldn't have kissed him, which was obviously what she was thinking. "When's he back?"

"Back? Oh, Chuck. Um, I'm not sure. I'll have to check the calendar. At home."

Lord, but she was a terrible actress. She wasn't much of a liar, either. He was amazed she'd fooled him for so long.

"Sure." He took a certain malicious glee in torturing her. He wasn't above punishing her for the suffering he'd already undergone because of her supposed marriage. "The reason I'm asking is I've got a date with a woman from Switzerland. I thought the four of us might go eat some fondue or something. Since you went to school in Switzerland, I think you two would hit it off." There was only one woman who interested him at the moment and if Jane called his bluff and took him up on his offer he was going to have to head over to the Swiss-Canadian friendship club and try to drum up a date. He wasn't too worried that the club would be called upon, however.

Her gaze widened, then faltered and he watched her twiddle her wedding ring nervously. Had her first reaction been jealousy? He hoped so. "A double date. My, that's a little..." She pushed at her hair, took a deep breath and said, "Can I get back to you?"

"Sure. Absolutely." He was slamming her against the wall and he didn't care. She had to come clean sooner or later and if he had anything to say about it, the truth-telling was going to happen soon. Very, very soon. "I'd like to get to know Chuck better. He seemed like a nice guy." It wasn't easy keeping the smirk off his face at her appalled expression.

"I know he felt the same way. But he doesn't have a lot of free time."

"No. Working in the entertainment industry must keep him busy." Chuck and Jane's Adventures in Marriage would provide enough entertainment to keep him amused for years if it weren't so damned pathetic. "Oh, well. Like I said. I'll fit in with your schedule."

He started for the door, but found suddenly he didn't have the stomach for any more teasing. He turned back and caught her looking vulnerable and confused. It was an act of will not to take the two steps necessary to pull her into his arms. Instead, he gave her the truth and hoped she'd reciprocate. "Jane, I won't apologize for last night, but I guess it's no secret I have...feelings for you. I know I've got no business having them. You're a married woman. That's the only reason I'm even considering seeing other women."

For a moment it seemed as though she'd tell him. He begged her with his eyes to come clean. "I'm..." she said, and faltered. "I'm not..." She stared at him, dropped her gaze to her ring and then clenched her fist. "Even if I weren't married, you'd still be my boss."

WHEN THE REQUEST came from Marsden Holt, it took Jane completely by surprise. She'd gone from optimistic to pretty much accepting of the fact that the firm would go with Graham's. She'd also accepted that Johnson the pervert would take the credit for all her work and there wasn't a thing she could do about it.

She was in the middle of wishing she could hurry up and get another job so she'd be free to tell Spence the truth when she answered her phone and heard the fatherly tones of John Marsden. After a few brief pleasantries, he came straight to the point.

"As you know, we'd pretty much decided to go with Graham's when you were representing that company." Marsden paused. "And I'll be honest, we looked at the Datatracker proposal more as a courtesy to you than with any serious intent." A sigh rumbled over the phone line. "But..."

Jane felt hope plummet at the "but". She'd so hoped she could persuade them to consider Datatracker. Since she'd been working with the company she'd come to respect the products and the people who made them. The competition between Datatracker and Graham's was classic David and Goliath stuff. She and

Spencer had given it their best with a slingshot, but it sounded as though Goliath had won this round. She dreaded seeing the disappointment on Spencer's face when she had to tell him the bad news.

"But, frankly, you and Spencer Tate made a very good presentation. And we like this new proposal enough that the purchasing committee is undecided. So we've agreed to give each company one last kick at the can. We'll schedule separate meetings with representatives of Graham and Sons and with you and Mr. Tate. We want to make a decision as soon as possible. Would it be convenient for you both to fly down next week?"

Jane's heart threatened to burst through her skull during the first part of his speech, then it sank like mercury in the Arctic when she realized they wanted her and Spencer to meet with them. Together.

Her limbs felt cold. Alicia might call her behavior cowardly, and that was when she was being nice, but Jane knew that the minute that ring came off, she'd be sleeping with her boss. She did not need the added enticement of staying in a hotel together.

To travel with him now would be horribly awkward for both of them. She fumbled with a pen, doodling on her Day-Timer, while she thought fast. "Um. I'll fly down of course, at your convenience. But Mr. Tate has a very busy schedule. I can't promise he'll be able to make it."

"Off the record Jane, we both know the Datatracker proposal wouldn't have made it this far without you. We have the highest opinion of your professionalism and salesmanship. But Datatracker doesn't have the history, the proven track record of Graham's. You're still the dark horse in this race. However, my colleagues were impressed that the CEO of the company came to help deliver the sales presentation. It made them feel more secure.

"Now I'm not telling you what to do, you understand. And I'm speaking out of turn to give you this much inside information. But Spencer Tate's presence at the meeting next week could tip the balance. I'm not saying it will, mind. But it could."

"I understand, Mr. Marsden. Believe me, I appreciate your honesty. I'll do my best."

"I know you will, Jane." Mr. Marsden's voice was warm. He was so nice. Just a decent man who ran a good company. And best of all he was at least sixty and happily married. Pictures of his grandchildren graced his desk. He was just the kind of boss Jane wanted.

She knew how much Spencer wanted this contract. He'd drop everything and jump at the chance. But she was too much of a salesperson to let the client know how eagerly Spencer wanted the account.

She'd planned to drop a delicate hint or two about how much she'd like to work for Marsden Holt, but somehow she hung up the phone without broaching the subject.

Jane was determined to nab that contract right from under that weasel Johnson's nose. Then she'd have paid off a score against that womanizing pervert.

And, if she gained a good client for Spence, she could leave Datatracker with a clean conscience.

So bagging Marsden Holt meant she'd have to spend

several days in Spencer's company fighting her own infatuation. She'd live.

She tried to ignore the anticipation zinging through her veins as she made her way to his office with the news.

She paused in the doorway, watching as he went over some papers with Yumi. His head was bent, his tousled hair flopped forward. She longed to comb it back off his forehead with her fingers. She told herself she didn't want to interrupt, but the truth was she enjoyed watching him. His rumpled shirt made her smile. He'd rolled the sleeves to his elbows and the desk lamp highlighted the coppery sheen glinting off the hair on his forearms. His muscular chest expanded and contracted with each breath.

Why couldn't he be sixty and have pictures of grandkids on his desk instead of being single and far too attractive for her peace of mind? No. Wait. She didn't want Spencer to be sixty and have grandkids. She wished instead that they'd met under other circumstances.

He looked up then and caught sight of her. Something flashed across his tired face—something vivid and alive that struck Jane like lightning and sizzled through her.

"Jane!" He smiled that dazzler of his and it was like the boom of thunder knocking her off her feet after the lightning had sizzled her insides to cinders.

She straightened from where she'd been leaning against the doorjamb mooning over him.

"Hi, Spencer." She cleared her throat. "Hi, Yumi. Don't let me interrupt. I can come back later."

Yumi looked back and forth between Jane and Spencer, an indulgent smile lifting the corners of her full red lips. "No problem. We were just about done. I'll make the changes and reprint it for your meeting, Spencer."

Yumi left.

Spencer'd loosened his tie, and it now hung crooked, giving a view of the hollow of his throat. A pulse beat clear and strong.

She wondered what he would do if she went over and pulled the tie the rest of the way off, then started on the buttons of his shirt. She imagined pulling the shirttails free and running her hands over his chest. She wouldn't kiss him, not yet. She'd start on her own buttons, then strip slowly until she could rub her aching breasts against the warm strength of his chest.

His dark eyes were getting darker, almost black. She felt as though he was reading her mind. She shook her head to get her thoughts back in order. "I...uh...I just talked to John Marsden. They've got to make a decision on their new system as soon as possible. They'd like us to meet with them next week."

Spencer jumped up out of his chair and approached her. "That's great."

She wasn't sure, but he looked as if he might be coming in for a bear hug.

She backed up a step. "We're not out of the woods yet. They're also scheduling a meeting with Graham's. Frankly, it will be a squeaker, but we've got a fighting chance."

"Fighting chance! We've got a better system, a more responsive support team, and I'm damn sure we're better priced." He grinned and her charred insides quivered to life again. "It'll be like shooting fish in a barrel."

"Minnows in the Atlantic. And I'm a terrible shot."

Spencer made a gun with his fingers, but whatever remark he was going to make was interrupted by the buzzing intercom. Yumi's voice warned him he had ten minutes until he was scheduled to meet his banker, which was at least a ten-minute car ride away.

He glanced at his watch and grimaced. "I've got to go. Can you set it up with Yumi? She knows all the details. I'll reschedule whatever I have to next week."

Jane nodded and began walking to the door.

"No." He stopped her. "You'll have more privacy in here." He called Yumi on the intercom and asked her to come in.

He started to drag his coat on and cursed as the sleeves caught on his rolled shirt. He yanked the sleeves down, buttoned the cuffs, and dragged the coat on again. His hopelessness made something warm and gooey happen to her insides. His tie was still crooked. "Spencer..." She should just tell him to fix his tie and comb his hair. But he looked at her and she gave into the need to get closer to him, to touch him, however briefly.

She moved forward. Took hold of his tie. As she slipped her hand under the knot to tighten it, the pulse in the hollow of his throat picked up its pace. She felt a similar quickening of her own pulse. The silk was warm under her hands and the underside of her fingers brushed his linen shirt. She felt the rough hair of his chest through the cloth.

She dropped her hands, dug into her suit pocket for

the small comb she always carried, and handed it to him silently.

While he combed his unruly hair, she took cover in scolding. "You should make sure and get your hair trimmed before you meet your banker. You know how conservative they are."

"Maybe I need someone to take care of me." He said it softly. His words snapped her gaze back to his face, where she read pain and longing. She licked dry lips unable to think of a thing to say. She was just standing there when Yumi knocked and, after a moment, entered.

"Sorry boss, but you gotta move. Here's the new printout of the financials. I called Harry in maintenance. He's bringing your car around to the front door. Good luck and get going."

He made a face at her, winked at Jane and grabbing his well-traveled briefcase, breezed out the door.

"Phew!" Jane said. "Is he always that slow?"

"He's worse when you're around."

Jane swung to look at Yumi who was smiling that smug, knowing smile of hers. Jane hoped she'd misunderstood. "What do you mean?"

"Come on, Jane. When you and Spencer look at each other I don't want to walk between you. I could get scorched."

Jane collapsed into one of the gray leather chairs and stared down at her clasped hands. "Nothing's going on between us."

Yumi's laugh was high-pitched, like birdsong. "You may not be doing anything. But plenty's going on."

"I don't know what to do."

The other woman sat across from Jane. "Why don't you start by telling him the truth?" Yumi's voice was soft as ever, but Jane heard steel in it.

She looked up sharply. "What truth?"

"You're not married to that guy you brought to the office party."

Guilt made Jane defensive. "What's this, your woman's intuition talking?"

Yumi shook her head. "The medical plan. When we sign you up for our company plan it automatically includes your spouse. You weren't in the office when I had to send the update in so I called the human resources department at your previous firm. There was no spouse."

"So I got married between jobs. It happens."

Yumi snorted. "Spencer may be too lovesick to see past his nose, but I'm not. If you ever walked down the aisle with that fellow you claimed as your husband, it was in a grocery store."

Jane clasped and unclasped her hands, her fake wedding ring a hard spot against the pliant flesh. "What are you going to do?"

"The question is, What are *you* going to do?" Yumi asked. "I like Spencer. He's a good boss and a fine man. I've been working for him for six years." Yumi's voice softened with affection. "He was so broken up when his wife left him, I worried about him. He got over her, but he never let himself get serious about any woman. Not 'till you. And it's eating him up inside. He sees you every day, but he thinks he can't have you. The thing is, I like you, too. I think you're perfect for Spencer. I don't want to see him hurt."

"I'm going to leave the company as soon as we land the Marsden Holt deal. I owe him that much," Jane said softly.

"Why don't you just get a divorce from Clark Gable?"

"Tom Cruise," Jane corrected automatically.

"You've got to be kidding."

"It's a long story."

Yumi shook her head. "And they call the Japanese inscrutable." She rose and went to Spencer's desk where she typed at the keyboard of one of his computers. "Here's his schedule for next week. Let's see...Monday's out, so's Tuesday. If you leave Wednesday after about 10:00 a.m. and skip the sales meeting Thursday, he's free until Monday. If you give me the information, I'll book your tickets and hotel."

"Thanks, Yumi." She flashed a grateful smile.

"You think about that divorce."

Jane nodded. "I will."

How could she explain her burning ambition to Yumi? Her whole life she'd been groomed to be the perfect wife to a rising young executive. And her whole life she'd fought to *be* that executive, to make a success or failure of her life on her own terms.

The irony of it was that she'd fallen for exactly the kind of man her parents would want her to marry. But it was impossible. Jane had a lot of plans to advance her career. Not one of them involved marrying the boss.

Not that anyone was talking marriage. Maybe a good healthy affair would get this thing out of their systems.

Jane wandered back to her office in a daze. She thought she'd kept her feelings completely to herself. If Yumi had noticed an attraction between her and Spencer, what were the rest of their colleagues thinking— and saying—behind her back?

12

"AND THAT'S another thing," Jane complained to Alicia on the phone that evening. "Everyone will say I'm sleeping with the boss to get ahead." She hadn't even stopped to change out of her suit. The minute she'd arrived home from work she'd phoned her best friend.

"Are you?"

"Of course not!"

"Well then, what's the big deal? People are always going to talk about something. This week it's you and Spencer, next week the rumor mill will pulverize somebody else. Your problem is you take things too seriously."

Jane kicked off her shoes. They fell to the carpet with hardly a thud. "Well, you certainly don't have that problem," she snapped. She hitched up her skirt and dragged off her nylons.

"Hey! Don't take it out on me!"

"Oh, Alicia. I'm sorry."

"What are you doing? You sound like you're inside a dryer."

Jane yanked and her head popped free of the silk noose she'd made of her chemise. "I'm changing. Always do two things at once, Time Management 101."

The receiver emitted a sound like a cat spitting up a furball. "Try Getting a Life 101."

Holding the receiver between her ear and shoulder,

Jane unzipped her skirt. "I'm just so mixed up I don't know what to do."

"Well two of the smartest women you know, me and Yumi, gave you the same advice. Doesn't that tell you something?"

"How do you know Yumi's smart? You've never met her."

"She has the opinions of an extremely intelligent woman," Alicia said firmly, and Jane couldn't help but smile.

"I'll think about it." Suddenly she wanted to talk about something other than her upcoming divorce from Tom Cruise. "So, how did your anniversary dinner go? Did our husband cheap out at the last minute and surprise you with the Golden Arches?"

"No. Il Paradiso, just as planned. And he surprised me with a diamond eternity ring."

Jane heard elation in Alicia's voice. Her black workout pants stalled at her knees. An eternity ring. She wondered what it would feel like to want to spend eternity with someone.

A picture of Spencer slipping a diamond-encircled band on her finger flashed through her mind. She knew just how his eyes would look: gentle and loving, with devil lights dancing in the background.

"Wow. Congratulations."

"I surprised him more, though. This is a secret for a few weeks yet, but I'm expecting a baby. I'm almost three months gone."

"Oh, Alicia. I'm so happy for you." A baby. A man to love for eternity. It had never sounded so good.

JANE HAD ASKED Yumi to book her on an earlier flight to Detroit than Spencer could take. She made excuses about needing extra time to prepare herself for the meeting, which they both knew she could just as easily have done in Vancouver.

Yumi gave her a You're-not-fooling-me look but booked the earlier flight.

Safely ensconced in her hotel room, Jane busied herself unpacking and pressing the wrinkles out of her best navy suit and white silk blouse.

Then she plugged in her laptop and reviewed the points she hoped to make in the next day's meeting.

Spencer was scheduled on an early-evening flight so Jane made sure she was out of the hotel before he arrived. The last time she'd been in this hotel, she mused, she'd been traveling with Johnson. She supposed it made sense for Yumi to book them here—it was the closest hotel to Marsden Holt—but she wished she'd requested different accommodations. She didn't like the mental associations.

She wandered downtown, window-shopping. She bought a paper from a street vendor and kept walking, looking for a restaurant she would feel comfortable eating in alone. She finally found a mid-priced Italian place offering brick-oven pizza made fresh on the premises.

She read the pizza selections and they made her mouth water, but there was something so pathetic about pizza for one. If ever there was a meal made for sharing, it was pizza. She opted instead for ravioli and salad.

It wasn't her first solitary dinner while on a business trip, but it was one of the loneliest. Probably because she kept thinking about Spencer, who most likely had expected her to eat with him. She bit her lip. If she and Spencer had gone out together, she'd have chosen Greektown, which she loved, but not on her own.

She forced herself to finish the pasta and salad and keep her eyes on the newspaper, which she scanned for the day's news and any mention of Marsden Holt.

After refusing dessert and coffee, Jane checked her watch. It was too early to go back to the hotel. She wanted an hour with Spencer before tomorrow's meeting. And not one minute more.

She remembered passing a movie theatre, so she strolled back the same way and took in a show. It was supposed to be a comedy, but it was way too mushy for Jane's taste. Where were the movies about women who didn't have to fall in love with a man to feel complete, she wondered as she rode the People Mover back to her hotel.

She was feeling irritated and unsettled when she walked back into the lobby a little after nine. She had to walk past the lobby bar to get to the elevator but was stopped by a sneering voice she knew too well.

"Lookee there. If it isn't little Jane Stanford trying to play in the big boys' league." She squinted into the dim bar and made out Phil Johnson with a nasty smirk on his face and, unless his habits had changed, a few drinks under his belt. She would have walked on without answering, if she hadn't happened to glance at his drinking companion.

Her eyes widened. Spencer was sharing a table with the man who'd managed to have her fired from her last job. As though reading her thoughts, Johnson continued.

"Your boss is lonely, honey. Why don't you come on over and warm him up?"

With a jerk, Spencer rose. "That's enough." He threw a couple of bills on the table and stalked toward Jane who still hadn't said a word. She didn't know whether he was angry with her or with Johnson but she wasn't waiting to find out which. She turned and continued walking to the elevator, forcing her legs to move at a normal speed when she wanted to sprint.

"Sleep well, you two." Johnson's voice carried easily across the quiet foyer.

Spencer caught up with Jane and they stalked in unison to the elevator. She didn't say anything until the doors slid shut. "Fraternizing with the enemy?" Her voice was icy. It was unfair, she knew. He couldn't know about her past. It wasn't unusual for competitors to get together socially when they found themselves in the same town. So long as they didn't talk shop, there was no harm done.

But, for some reason, seeing Spencer with that slime Johnson infuriated Jane. She did see Johnson as the enemy. He was a small, weak man who couldn't bear to let a woman get ahead.

"I was waiting for you to show up. Didn't they teach you in finishing school that it's polite to leave a message if you're not having dinner with your traveling companion?"

Jane swung around, surprised by the flinty blackness of his eyes. She'd avoided him. So what? She'd been avoiding him for weeks. Why did he have to call her on it now? His anger fueled her own. "You're not my traveling companion. You're my boss. And outside of office hours my time is my own."

He stepped closer, crowding her in the small elevator. The endearing boyishness was gone. His jaw was as hard as Stonehenge, his attitude from the same era. "I wanted to go over the presentation notes. You didn't answer your phone, I couldn't find you in the restaurant—"

A spurt of red-hot anger flamed up inside her, partly due to guilt. "You and Johnson looked perfectly cozy without me."

The hollow ping of the elevator signaled her floor. She stormed out, Spencer stomping right behind her.

He grabbed her arm and hauled her around to face him.

"I was sitting alone watching the lobby for you. Johnson came and sat with me. Uninvited. And believe me, unwelcome. I only let him sit down to find out if he knew where you were. I wanted to get your opinion on my talking points for tomorrow."

She looked at him and saw a wealth of emotion there that confused as well as drew her. It wasn't the notes he'd been so anxious to see. It was her. She lowered her voice with an effort. "I should have left a message. I'm sorry."

If he'd left things there, it would have ended. But he didn't. "I'd appreciate a message next time. You're a woman alone in a strange city. I'm responsible for—"

"No." She jabbed him in the chest with her index finger. Why had she ever thought he was a modern, enlightened man? The man was a total Neanderthal. Outside of office hours she didn't answer to him or anyone. The anger that had dimmed flared again at his arrogance. "I am responsible for myself. Just me. No one else. Can you get that through your prehistoric pea brain? You employ me. You don't own me." She continued to punctuate her words with pokes to his chest.

He grabbed her hand away from his chest and held on to it when she tried to tug it out of his grasp. "I was worried. Can you get that through *your* dogmatic feminist brain? Is it a crime to care?"

His words echoed in her brain. The sweet, rockheaded Neanderthal cared.

About her.

As hard as she tried to keep up her righteous indignation, she was touched.

He was still holding her hand. Hard. As though he'd never let it go.

And, as she looked into the deep-brown eyes, the bitter truth struck Jane. He could drag her off to his cave without having to use a cudgel or even pull her hair.

She was tired of proving how great she was alone. If only she could harness his strength....

Her eyes wandered over the rugged face, the strong jaw, sensitive lips.

Her heart was beginning to pound. She licked dry lips.

She felt the tug on her hand. "Jane?" His voice was a ragged whisper.

She moved slowly toward him, rising on tiptoe to reach his lips with her own. He didn't move away, but didn't lean forward, either. She could tell how much he wanted her. It was in his eyes and the way his breathing had stalled, but if she wanted to kiss him, she was on her own.

Maybe it was her diatribe about being in control of her own life, but he clearly wasn't going to hit on her, in spite of the pent-up need pulling them together. He wanted her to seduce him.

The knowledge gave her a feeling of power that was amazingly erotic. He might be the boss back at the office, but he was making it clear that here and now, she was the boss. As much as he wanted her, the next move was hers.

The attraction that had been building steadily since she'd first seen him was too strong for her to fight anymore. Whatever the consequences to her career, she was a woman—and Spencer was the man she wanted. Needed, actually. Quite desperately. She was so caught up in the moment and in her needs as a woman, that her career goals seemed suddenly insignificant. Getting involved with Spence was going to have repercussions, she realized dimly as she felt the warmth of his hand around hers and the mesmerizing pull of his mouth.

The hell with the repercussions.

She brushed her lips across his, a light fluttering touch that tormented them both. His lips were warm and firm beneath hers, but as she pulled away she heard the sharp hiss of air through his teeth. Just that fleeting touch, and his reaction, started her trembling.

Licking her lips, she glanced up into his eyes and saw the strength of his desire blazing in their depths as they followed the motion of her tongue. Against the force of his gaze, her self-control shattered into a million pieces.

She lunged.

Digging her fingers into the untamed mess of his hair she dragged his head down even as she raised her face to meet his. She was just so tired of common sense, of squelching her femininity and her woman's needs. Just this once, she had to let go, give in to wild, restless urges that had nothing to do with common sense. Then their lips met, and all conscious thought fled.

This time, he took part in the kiss.

His arms came around her, warm and strong, pulling her up against his body. His lips, those tender-strong incredible lips that could laugh at her or frown in irritation at her independent nature, kissed her with such ruthless determination that she could hardly keep her feet under her.

She felt the last vestiges of his anger in that kiss, in the commanding way he took possession of her mouth.

She opened her lips, needing more of him, and his tongue plunged inside. She moaned at the incredible sensations swirling through her, and he dragged her even tighter against him until she could feel every line of his muscular build. One line in particular was making its presence felt and its intention clear.

She pressed her hips against him, rubbing herself against his erection until he groaned. She felt the slickness of her own arousal, wanting him so badly she literally ached. Her hands moved feverishly over his body stroking the shifting muscles of his back, grasping his firm, round butt.

The ping of the elevator made her pull back with a gasp.

She tried to struggle free of his hold, but he didn't let go, merely manhandled her into an alcove. In the dim light from the soda dispenser, she gazed at Spencer, who was panting and staring right back at her with all the wanting showing. The humming ice machine had nothing on her, running hot and cold at the same time. Her heart hammered wildly. What was she doing?

She heard the footsteps and muted voices of a couple walking down the corridor. She jerked out of Spencer's arms, and this time he let her go.

He didn't say a word, just kept gazing at her with eyes that telegraphed *I want you*. She didn't dare hold his gaze, knowing her own eyes were sending the same message. She focused on the sparkling ice cubes in the machine. Automatically, she tidied her hair with her fingers. And, darn it, they were shaking. This was a business associate she was throwing herself at. She forced her mind to concentrate on business.

Feeling as though she needed to stick her head in the ice cubes until her common sense returned, she said, "I'm sorry. That was totally unprofessional behavior."

A disbelieving snort was her only reply.

Out of the corner of her eye, she watched Spence shove his hands in his pockets as though to keep them out of trouble.

Business. She had to think about business. "Seeing as Johnson is here, I suppose they booked both meetings the same day?" she said, trying not to pant.

Spencer nodded. "Graham and Sons meet them at

nine tomorrow morning. We're on the agenda after lunch."

She summoned a bright smile. "Wonderful. We can meet over breakfast and talk strategy without fear of anyone from Graham's overhearing us." She dug in her purse for her room key. "I'm going to review my notes one more time. I'll see you in the morning."

He reached for her, but stopped in midmotion. "This is not over."

"It is for tonight."

His eyes narrowed, then he nodded abruptly. "Sleep well."

It was great advice, but she had trouble following it. Her pillow was lumpy, her mattress too hard, the air conditioner too noisy.

And her body, too damned on edge.

She flung the covers away in frustration. That kiss had her so fired up she could hardly stand it. She wanted him here, in her bed, fulfilling all the promises his eyes and his lips and his hands had made. If only she'd met Spencer Tate on a golf course, or at a party. Even if he were a colleague she could probably allow herself to give in to the mutual attraction. But he wasn't just a colleague, he was her boss.

And Jane Stanford wasn't about to sleep with her boss.

She got up, padded to the bathroom, drank some cold water, and stared at her strained face in the mirror. They needed to win this account tomorrow. The ring on her finger glinted and she frowned down at it.

She was never going to sell anything to anybody if she didn't get some sleep. She stomped over to the air conditioner and flicked it off, then dragged herself back to bed and tried to beat the lumpy pillow into submission. She closed her eyes and willed herself to sleep.

"Sleep well." His words echoed in her mind, an edge of derision to them. He'd as good as told her he wouldn't be sleeping well. Maybe he'd known she wouldn't be either.

She enjoyed the blissful silence without the air conditioner for a good fifteen minutes before the air started getting stuffy. And it was hot. Or was that just her overheated body?

"This is ridiculous!" she cried aloud in the dark. She was single; he was single. She was attracted to him; he was attracted to her. She knew what room number he was in. Yumi had made sure of it.

She was going to march right to his door and put them both out of their misery.

Jane's body yearned for him. She'd never in her life experienced a wanting like this. He was one floor down, a few rooms over. She pictured him lying in a big empty bed staring up at the ceiling. Was his pillow as pummeled? His bedding as tortured?

What was the big deal? Why shouldn't she, just once in her life, throw caution to the wind? Jump into bed with a man she was wildly attracted to? She threw the covers back again, jumped out of bed and dragged on a terry-cloth robe with the hotel logo on the pocket. Who was she going to run into in the corridor at two in the morning? Besides, she didn't want to mess around dressing and undressing.

She wanted to be with Spencer.

Naked.

And very soon.

She almost ran back into the bathroom, where she brushed her teeth and fluffed her hair. She applied a little lipstick then rubbed it off. Instead she brushed just a hint of blush on her pale cheeks and made one quick sweep with the mascara brush. Satisfied, she left the bathroom and drew a deep breath.

And got as far as the door.

Her hand was on the knob when she stopped dead.

Go, go, her body urged.

Don't be a fool. He's your boss, her reason counseled.

She wavered. Her body trembled with need. She'd never felt so conflicted, or so unsure of herself. She wanted him with a physical force that frightened her. She wanted to do every sexual thing she'd ever heard of with him. She wanted to touch him and taste him, to meld her body with his. She turned the doorknob.

But her mind had ruled supreme for too many years. Her reason sent out arguments like distress flares exploding behind her eyelids. *He's your boss. You love your career. Don't be a slut.* The last one lit up her mother's face along with the words.

With a groan, she sank to the floor, leaning against the door. How could she throw herself at him tonight, as a lover, and act like a professional tomorrow morning?

Worse still, what if she got to his door and he was sleeping, or refused her advances? She would die on the spot of humiliation. And Johnson would walk right over her dead body and win the Marsden Holt account.

She dragged herself back to bed one last time. When she pulled the covers up she discovered she was trembling.

It was a very long night.

13

JANE LOOKED like hell, Spence thought smugly when he met her for breakfast the next morning. Well, as much as a woman so naturally stunning could look like hell, he amended.

"Sleep in?" she asked, hopefully he thought. It was clear from her pale skin and the dark smudges under her eyes that she hadn't slept well. No doubt she'd be pleased if she knew he'd suffered the same fate. But he had his pride. Fortunately, he could fake looking well-rested better than she. He'd been known to go twenty-four hours at a stretch when he was immersed in product design and engineering. In fact, he could manage for weeks on end with only a few hours each night.

So, though he'd had almost no sleep either he ran his fingers through his still-damp hair and said. "No. I slept fine. I was working out." For two solid hours, but she didn't need to know that.

She'd kissed him and then dumped him on his ass last night, within view of the night of pleasure he'd longed for since the moment she'd first walked into his office. She'd hurt his pride. There was no reason she should know she'd also robbed him of sleep.

It was beginning to occur to Spencer that Jane Stanford was one bizarre woman. She lied about her marital status, denied a perfectly healthy sexual attraction and acted like an outraged nun because of one kiss.

Yes, she was beautiful. Painfully so, but he didn't care about that. He'd thought he wanted the passionate woman he believed lurked inside those navy suits and endless buttons. Now he wasn't so sure. Perhaps he'd projected his own hot desires onto an essentially cold woman.

In any case, a man could take only so much punishment. They had a presentation to make. If sex happened between them, great. If it didn't, there were other interesting and attractive women in the world. What Jane had done was to remind him once again that he had to get out more and meet some of those women.

Sure, some would be disasters, like the chain-smoking hyena and the anorexic calorie-phobic model, but some would turn out to be perfectly nice. And somewhere out there was the woman he'd marry eventually, settle down with and raise a family. Hell, he was getting to the age where coaching Little League and owning a collie and a station wagon sounded good.

So he took the high road—pretended that there had been no kiss last night and they were here for business and business only. If she expected any more attempts to break down her defenses and get the truth out of her, the woman was going to be disappointed. She could keep her phony ring, her phony husband and her phony life. He was looking for a flesh-and-blood woman with the guts to face up to her needs.

Having decided all that, he had to squelch the impulse to lean over and take her hand. She looked so damned tired and unsure of herself.

"Nervous about the presentation?"

She smiled faintly. "Not really."

"Good. We've got time to go through a last complete run-through. Then, we roll."

Sure, Jane thought. If she were rolling, it was the way a slug might roll up a hill. Usually she was good at focusing, but between her lack of sleep and Spencer's disturbing presence, she could only stumble her way through her Power Point practice presentation. He, on the other hand, made *her* want to go out and buy one of the Datatracker systems.

However, just as a disastrous dress rehearsal is supposed to predict a successful opening night at the theater, so her lousy practice seemed to galvanize her when it counted.

Maybe she didn't put on the best presentation of her life once she and Spencer got to Marsden Holt, but it was right up there. Somehow, while her boss had distracted her when they were alone, he was a comforting presence in the big board room where all the MH decision makers had gathered.

This was her chance, not only to help sell the Datatracker system, but to make a good enough impression that she could maybe get a job here, one that would save both herself and Spencer the awkwardness of trying to combine a work and a personal relationship. She wasn't just saving her own reputation, she told herself, but Spencer's as well. If a soft, but obnoxious voice—sounding a lot like Alicia's—intruded to tell her she was running away, she ignored it.

This was it. She knew it, Spencer knew it, every person in the room knew it. Because they'd all seen the specs and read the reports, she focused briefly on the top sales points—the areas she knew Datatracker was strongest in and the areas in which Graham's tended to be weaker.

Spence, as in their earlier meeting, relied on a spontaneous speech that described his company, the pride they took in their products, and some of their successes. He was so damned likeable, he managed to get the room laughing on several occasions.

As she sat back and watched him field questions, she felt proud of him. She knew they'd done their best and that they deserved this contract, but it was impossible to read how the vote would go once the presentation was over, the questions asked and answered and they were being thanked for their time.

"We'll be in touch soon," John Marsden said as he showed them out and shook their hands, as genial as ever.

"I am so glad that's over," she said as they rode back to the hotel in a cab. Now that her adrenaline level had ebbed, she realized she was hungry and it was past lunchtime. She waited for Spence to suggest they share a meal, maybe even ask the cab to drop them at a restaurant, but he didn't.

They made it all the way back to their hotel by talking about the presentation and trying to guess who'd been on their side and who'd be more likely to be swayed by the larger, more established firm.

Once the cab dropped them off, Spence said, "Well,

I'm going to call into the office and see what's up. I think my flight leaves about six. How about yours?"

"We're on the same flight, actually." She couldn't blame him for asking, since she'd purposely taken a separate flight down.

"Fine. See you later."

He turned and strode away. She stood rooted to the spot. So, she'd be eating lunch on her own. Fine. She couldn't blame him for not suggesting a meal together when she'd been so vehement about her personal time last night. Still, he could have suggested they share a cab to the airport, couldn't he?

SPENCER TOSSED socks at his open overnight bag. Both black balls ended in rimshots and bounced back on the bed.

He frowned at the bag, the jumble of clothing inside. With all the practice he'd had, his aim should be perfect. How many years had he been doing this—going from town to town, pushing his products, himself, the reputation of his company?

He remembered when he had been free to design computer systems. Clever arrangements that made information tracking and retrieval smoother for big companies. He was a wunderkind, one of those brainy young hackers who didn't know what the limits were and so blew them all away. And it didn't matter if he wore socks at all.

He was so good he'd ended up with his own company. And then he didn't have time to design anymore. Nowadays he was an administrator and salesman. His most complex design was his Day-Timer.

He sank to the bed and sat staring at the geometric patterns in the carpet. He thought back to the meeting this afternoon, when he'd fielded some of the technical questions, how he'd relished the chance to explain the internal architecture to the two technicians who could appreciate it. If it hadn't been for Jane's smooth intervention, the suits would have fallen dead on the floor, stiff with boredom. The truth was, he was a true blue computer nerd, promoted out of what he did best and loved most.

Even the designs on the carpet reminded him of circuit boards. He wished he could go back to what he loved best. Then he wouldn't have to travel so much. He'd be able to spend more time at home, maybe get married again. Trade the apartment for a real home.

The instant he imagined a home, he pictured Jane in it. So much for his pious BS at breakfast. He didn't want any nice woman. Who was he kidding? He wanted Jane. Why the hell wouldn't she tell him the truth? She was crazy about him, about as crazy as he was for her. Why not just say, "Spencer, I'm single, let's get naked." How hard was that?

He'd left her with her finishing-school-trained mouth hanging half-open when he'd dumped her in the lobby. Ha. If she wanted to play hardball with his emotions, she was going to have to accept that he could play rough, too.

He got up, shoved the sock balls into the case, glanced round the room and spotted a running shoe in one corner. He found the second under the bed and rammed them in the top of the bag. With one hand he

forced the lumpy contents down while he dragged the
zipper shut with the other.

He wished his desires could be shut away as easily.
Jane was driving him crazy. He wanted her as he'd
never wanted anything. That wild kiss against the pop
machine last night had told him she wanted him, too.

If they hadn't been interrupted, the night might have
ended a lot differently.

Something had to give. He decided to have it out
with her when they got back to Vancouver. Tell her his
feelings, put his heart on the line. The idea scared the
hell out of him, but he couldn't go on like this, letting
her pathetic lie keep them apart....

14

THE RING of the telephone jarred Spencer out of his reverie. His heart picked up speed. Jane?

After the way he'd unceremoniously left her in the lobby, he didn't think so. Probably Yumi.

He picked up the phone. "Spencer Tate."

"Spencer, glad I caught you. John Marsden here."

"Yes, John?" He tried to sound casual, but he crossed his fingers and twisted his left leg around his right—a superstitious hangover from childhood.

"I'll get right to the point. I'm calling with good news. The contract is yours."

He held down a whoop of excitement, settled for a soundless one-armed drum roll on the bed. "That's great news." He was proud of how cool he sounded. "You've made the right decision."

"We think so, too. We'd like to make the formal announcement tomorrow morning at the plant. I just called on the off chance you and Jane could stay an extra night and help present the system to our employees."

Spencer had reams of work waiting back at the office. The last thing he could afford was another day away. "Sure," he heard himself say. "I'll do some rescheduling. No problem."

"I tried to call Jane and tell her, but she's not in her room. Would you mind giving her the good news?"

"Not at all."

There was a pause, as though the man at the other end was debating his next words. Finally he said, "She's a fine salesperson. If I wasn't an honorable man I'd try and steal her from you."

Something about the choice of words made Spencer's gut tighten. He wished Jane was his. Not his employee...just his. Then nobody, but nobody, would ever get a chance to steal her away.

He forced himself to sound casual. Even managed a chuckle. "Thanks for the reminder. I'll make sure she gets a generous bonus."

He dialed Jane's room as soon as he got Marsden off the phone, but she still wasn't answering. He left a message for her that they were staying another night. Then he called Yumi and had her reschedule their flights. He called the front desk to extend the booking on his room and Jane's.

Then he called the concierge to get a reservation at the top-rated restaurant in Detroit and reserved dinner for two. *If I wasn't an honorable man...* The words haunted him. He'd always thought of himself as an honorable man. Tried hard to be one. An intimate dinner for two had *seduction* written all over it.

With a sigh, he picked up the phone again and managed to reach Marsden. "Jane and I would like to invite you and your wife to dinner tonight to celebrate the news and thank you for your business."

It was quickly arranged and the dinner reservation amended to four.

He tried Jane's room again and this time she answered on the first ring. All the woman had to do was say "hello" and he felt a hot rush of pleasure. If she ever talked dirty in his ear he'd probably explode.

"It's Spencer—"

"Spencer. I got your message. I've been trying your line for ages. What's up?"

The excitement in her tone made him smile his own triumph. "We did it!"

Since she didn't have to act dignified with him as he'd had to do with Marsden, she got to yell in his ear. "That's fantastic! I thought we had them, just at the end, when you agreed to throw in an extra year's technical support. But I wasn't sure."

"They want us to be on hand for the big announcement tomorrow. I agreed. Is that okay?"

"Yes, of course. I'd left a couple of free days in my schedule anyway, just in case." She sounded breathless, as though she'd been running.

"Since I couldn't get hold of you, I went ahead and made reservations for a celebration dinner with Marsden and his wife. Will you be available to join us?" He tried to keep his tone neutral. Evenings were her free time as she'd made sure to let him know. But even to his own ears his voice sounded childish.

She gave a low whistle when he mentioned the restaurant. "Of course I can make it. On your expense account, I hope."

He chuckled, feeling his annoyance drain away as anticipation took its place. Maybe it wouldn't be an intimate dinner for two, but at least they would be having dinner together. He waited a moment. If she was at all like every woman he'd ever met he knew what was coming next. She didn't disappoint him.

"But, Spencer. All I have with me is business suits. I didn't bring a single dress."

"You can use some of the generous bonus you earned and go shopping."

"What do you mean a bonus?"

"Marsden talked me into it. He said if he wasn't an honorable man, he'd steal you. So, being an astute businessman, I'm bribing you to stay with Data-tracker."

He'd meant it as a joke, expected her to laugh, but she was strangely quiet. The silence made him feel uneasy. Surely she couldn't be stolen from Datatracker—could she?

"Jane? You still there?"

"Yes, yes I'm still here. I can't believe it." She gave a shaky laugh. "It better be a big bonus. I only have time to go to the lobby shops with the exorbitant prices."

"Buy ten dresses. You earned them."

IN THE END she bought only one. But it was the price of ten. A stunning cocktail-length sheath in cornflower-blue silk that did things for her eyes. And her figure.

The dress wasn't revealing—it was a business dinner after all—but it was feminine, and it fitted as though it had been custom-made for her. The store just happened to stock the perfect bag—a beaded blue evening clutch—as well as matching shoes and just the right lingerie.

She tried not to blanch when she handed over her gold card, restrained herself from snatching it back when she heard the electronic babble from the little machine confirming the purchase.

The effusive clerks referred her next door for designer costume jewelry. She hesitated, then marched over.

A dress like that cried out for the full treatment—hair, facial, manicure—but she didn't have time. She did her best with her hair, pinning it up a bit more elaborately than usual and leaving a few curls to spill free. She also spent much longer than usual on her makeup.

She tried to persuade herself she wanted to make a good impression on John Marsden and his wife, but deep down she knew for whom she was dressing.

She was only human. Perversely, the minute Spencer had taken her broad hint and started treating her as no more than an employee, she'd realized how much she'd enjoyed the slight intimacy they'd shared. She had to stop being such a coward. It was time to tell him the truth and take a chance. Maybe, if they were very, very discreet, no one would ever know.

Jane arrived first at their assigned meeting place in the lobby. She felt as though it were prom night and she was wearing her first corsage as she searched out Spencer among the hordes of people coming and going. She put the most forbidding expression she could manage on her face but it didn't stop men from staring at her. After an offer to buy her a drink, she wished she were wearing the most conservative business suit she owned.

She breathed a sigh of relief when she caught sight of Spencer gliding down the escalator, and her heart hiccupped. Then it started beating double-time. He looked wickedly desirable in a charcoal evening suit and crisp white shirt. His hair was perfectly groomed but for one little tuft sticking out just behind his left ear. His eyes scanned the foyer with an earnest expression. He looked right at her and her poor heart lurched again.

Then his dark gaze swept past her without a pause, and her welcoming smile dimmed. She felt as though she'd just wasted a small fortune.

He strode through the crowd toward their meeting place and only when he was almost on top of her did he glance her way again. His reaction was a classic double-take. She saw his eyes widen and his jaw drop. With a pleased inward smile, she re-evaluated the small fortune she'd spent in the hotel lobby. Now it seemed like a bargain.

Cinderella at the ball.

Prince Charming struck dumb, his gorgeous mouth hanging open.

Yes!

"Wow!" he said.

It wasn't the most elegant compliment she'd ever received, but it was one of the most flattering.

"Wow yourself," she answered, letting her gaze traverse the perfect cut of the suit, one she'd never seen before. "Somebody else got a bonus, I see."

"Why do women always think they're the only ones who like to shop?" His mouth pulled tight in a mock frown, but his eyes were twinkling and the way they were looking at her made her body feel warm all over.

"Don't tell me you're a secret shopaholic, Spencer?"

"I'm not telling you my secrets. Not yet anyway."

The good-natured bantering continued as he took her elbow and led her through the big brass doors, and it seemed they'd both dropped their pretense of non-attraction. However, the mood stayed light and casual during the cab ride to the restaurant. It made a great cover for the awareness Jane felt of her companion as a man in his sexual prime. Behind the boyish charm that never failed to lower her guard, she kept glimpsing the grown man, and his grown-up desires.

Underneath her light chatter, her pulse drummed out a lightning-fast salsa.

When they reached the restaurant, they were led to a table for four in a quiet corner. They had deliberately arrived early to welcome their guests, so it was no surprise that the table was empty.

After they settled themselves the waiter arrived, greeting them with a strong French accent. "Would you care for a drink to begin with, *monsieur et madame?*" His assumption that they were man and wife gave Jane a secret thrill.

Spencer looked at Jane. "Champagne?"

"Mmm." She nodded.

"Crystal if you have it."

The waiter looked as though he'd been struck. He stared down his long nose at them. "But of course we have it. We stock seventeen varieties of champagne." He dragged the last word out for about ten minutes.

The man stalked away and Spencer's lips twitched.

"I think you've made an enemy for life," Jane murmured.

She looked up to see John Marsden and a pleasant-faced woman approaching the table and she and Spence rose to shake hands.

She'd always liked John Marsden, so it was no trial to spend the evening with the man. He was courteous and formal; his wife, both elegant and sweet.

For a business dinner, Jane had to admit, it was a roaring success. Not in the least because there was a very unbusinesslike undercurrent buzzing between her and Spence. When his glance rested on her it scorched.

What was happening between them was magnetic and, she now realized, inevitable.

It wasn't just the champagne fizzing in her veins as she and Spencer made the return cab ride to the hotel. It was white-hot desire. Gone was the careful banter. Instead they were both silent.

She glanced at her companion from under her lashes. His expression was serious. He stared at his locked hands as though debating something with himself.

Yumi's words echoed in her head and she felt a sharp stab of guilt. Was she causing him pain? She was certainly feeling it. Never in her life had she met a man who could make her sizzle with just a look. Why did it have to be the one man who could destroy her career?

She turned to stare out the window. She caught glimpses of the Detroit River. They passed through the downtown area with its skyscrapers and a few older, more squat stone and brick buildings. Reviewing her dull and mostly nonexistent sex life, Jane saw a pattern she'd never noticed before. She dated men who were boring, predictable, like Owen who, as Alicia liked to remind her, was more interested in fish guts than women.

All her life she'd steered a wide path around men like Spencer: up-and-coming success stories, men who commanded and controlled. She was afraid to lose control. Afraid to end up in the life her mother had so carefully planned for her from birth. But Spencer made her question her own assumptions. With him she wanted to lose control. Just once, she wanted to let passion, instead of reason, dominate her actions. And what harm could there be in that? She'd done what she'd set out to do. She'd won the Marsden Holt account. Soon she'd leave Datatracker anyway.

She turned to Spencer and found him gazing at her with such hunger in his eyes that her overworked heart jumped again.

"You look beautiful tonight." His voice was a low whisper.

His face was serious, his dark-brown eyes almost black in the darkness of the cab. She heard the silk of her gown rustle as she moved, without thought, toward him.

The cab stopped with a jerk, bringing her up short. She glanced up, startled, to see the hotel doorman opening the cab door for her. She stood aside as Spencer threw money into the cab driver's hand, slipped something to the doorman, grabbed her hand and almost sprinted toward the hotel doors.

Hand in hand they moved through the quiet lobby to the elevator. They didn't speak, except through the urgent heat running back and forth between their clasped hands. She pushed the button for her own floor and he seemed content to let her lead. She needed at least this much control, to take him to her room.

Their hands stayed fused until they reached her door when she pulled away to take her keycard out of the glitter clutch. Her hand trembled so he took the card from her, opened the door and held it while she entered.

The room was dimly lit by a single bedside lamp. The air conditioner hummed quietly. The bed was turned down on both sides, like a sign, and a wrapped mint winked from each pillow.

The click of the door closing behind her seemed ridiculously loud. She turned.

She'd managed to avoid looking at him since he'd taken her hand. Now, she raised her gaze to his. He still looked solemn, and much larger than usual. She'd taken the lead this far. Now she couldn't move, could only stare into those dark, dark eyes.

She could swear he was waiting for something, and in that instant she knew what she had to do.

Divorce Tom Cruise.

15

"SPENCER, my marriage was a...mistake." A lie was what it was, but she couldn't bring herself to tell him that. "It's over." The words felt odd, foreign to her, and she realized how much she hated the idea of failing at marriage—even though it was a pretend marriage and a pretend divorce.

She thought she saw a gleam of irritation in his eyes, but realized she must be mistaken. It had been so long since she'd slept with anyone she'd probably forgotten what hot desire looked like.

"Have you left him?" he asked.

Of course, he was an honorable man. She'd liked that about him from the beginning. He wouldn't want to sleep with a married woman. She cringed in shame. He must think she was a faithless slut. Which was the biggest joke of the century. She hadn't had sex in almost two years and he thought she was juggling two men. She licked her lips, knowing he'd leave if she didn't come clean. Well, partly clean. "Yes. I did."

Okay, unbelievably lame. She tried again. "I mean, we're separated. I'm living alone."

He appeared to consider her words with great solemnity. "Any chance of a reconciliation?"

The idea of her and Chuck spending their lives together made her shudder. "No!"

He stepped closer and lifted his hand to her cheek. She closed her eyes and felt his fingers feather over her face. She felt them pause under her chin and raise it. Still with her eyes closed, she felt his warmth, sensed his lips coming closer. He smelled citrusy and clean.

Then his lips touched hers, soft and feather-light. She sensed his hesitancy, felt the internal struggle. It could be a good-night kiss, or it could flame into something more.

He lifted his head. She could not bear it if he left her now. With a tiny sigh, she reached up into the thick waves of hair at the back of his head and pulled him back to her.

She heard his moan of surrender and this time his kiss was fierce, almost angry in its intensity. He pulled her hard against him and she heard the rustle of silk as her dress crushed between them. As the kiss deepened, so did her need. She felt her body crying out for fulfillment in every dark, secret place.

His tongue was demanding as it took possession of her mouth, stroking, exploring, stoking the fire. She tasted champagne, wanted to taste all of him.

She pressed closer, flattening her aching breasts against his chest. He seemed to understand her need, for he reached for the back of her dress, found the hook at the top and then she heard the slow, slithering hiss of her zipper.

Raising his head he took a step backwards and her dress began to slide. She bent forward to grab it back.

"Leave it," he commanded.

And she did. She stood there while the dress whispered its way down her length to languish at her feet.

His gaze moved slowly from her hair, still pinned up, down her body to the sea of filmy blue that swirled round her ankles. It took an effort of will to stop herself from crossing her hands over her breasts.

She was wearing the silky lingerie in smoky-blue lace and satin but she felt naked beneath his gaze. He was backlit by the bedside lamp so his face was shadowy and mysterious, while she felt far too exposed in the barely-there lingerie. She hadn't bothered with stockings, making do with a pedicure and strappy shoes.

It seemed an eternity that he stood there, fully dressed and motionless. Finally his lips moved. "You look like Venus, rising from the sea."

It seemed an appropriate image, the birth of the love goddess, for there was something brand-new about the way she was feeling, the things she wanted.

He moved suddenly to shuck his jacket. He tossed it to the floor and Jane fought the urge to rescue it. His shirt followed and then she didn't care anymore about creases or slovenly habits. She just stared at him. His chest was sculpted and athletic, his waist flat. The muscles of his belly filled her with lust. Odd, she'd never had that reaction before. She fixed her attention on it. A dark line of hair led down into the waistband of his trousers, but her gaze followed the line up to the swirls of dark hair on his chest.

She stepped out over the folds of her dress, careful not to catch the silk in her heels and while her inner good girl nagged at her to hang the outrageously expensive gown properly, her inner bad girl said, *the hell with it*. For once, her inner bad girl won.

She closed the distance between them, lifted her hands to his chest and let her fingers slip through the coarse, curling hair.

Oh, he smelled so good, and his skin was warm.

Still, she shivered.

Spence took hold of her arms and squeezed gently. "Are you sure about this?"

"Yes. I'm getting a divorce." It came out in a hoarse croak.

"I don't want you doing anything you'll regret."

How could she begin to explain her feelings? She stepped away from the distraction of his arms, sank to the bed and twiddled the gold band on her finger. How could she possibly make him understand about her absurd faux marriage? "The whole thing was a bad mistake." She thought about Johnson, and Alicia's warning and shook her head, wondering how she could have been so blind. "I never remember showing such poor judgment."

Since she was currently staring at the floor, she saw his feet, still in their shiny black shoes, cross the carpet toward her. The mattress beside her sagged as he sat beside her and his arm came around her shoulders, warm and comforting. He was going to be understanding about this. She sighed with relief.

"A divorce is pretty serious stuff." A frown appeared between his brows. "Are you sure?"

She couldn't tell him she'd made the whole thing up—couldn't risk his outrage, his condemnation. Even worse, the possibility that he'd walk right out of her hotel room and leave her here, wanting him.

She'd make sure he never found out. She'd probably

be moving soon to another job anyway. She just wanted this one night with this special man. Was that so terrible?

"Yes. Chuck knows it could never work between us," she answered, stifling a nervous giggle as she wondered how Chuck would phrase a suggestion that he and Jane spend their lives together. "My marriage is over."

He took a deep breath. "Do you want to talk about it?"

Talk? Her body was screaming out for fulfillment. Talk was the last thing she wanted. She didn't want a sensitive new-age guy. She wanted the Neanderthal back.

Jane sucked in a deep breath, realizing she was going to have to take matters back into her own hands.

She turned her head, letting her gaze meet his. "No," she whispered. "I don't want to talk."

Slowly, she twisted the gold ring off her finger, and he watched intently. She stood up, walked into the bathroom and dropped the ring on the counter where it clinked against her toiletry bag and nudged her brain so she dug through the bag.

Jane liked to travel prepared for most emergencies. In a special pouch were the least likely supplies she'd ever need. She dug past her water-purification tablets and the letter indicating her parents' address, to three packs of condoms. She hoped they hadn't disintegrated with old age.

With a deep breath, she thrust her shoulders back and looked at herself in the mirror. She felt foolish, sexy and absolutely determined. She headed back into the bedroom and her spirits rose when she saw Spencer still sitting on the bed. He hadn't moved, not even to take off his shoes. But he hadn't put his shirt back on either. And he hadn't left while she was in the bathroom.

She tried to act casual and sophisticated as she dropped the plastic trio on the nightstand, but she felt her cheeks heating. He watched her silently until she turned back to him.

"You're sure about this?" His voice was gruff.

She didn't want him to be calm and reasonable and ask stupid questions. No. She wasn't sure. But her body was. Achingly so. She nodded and moved toward him. She sank to her knees and bent to unlace his shoes. Then she removed them. She peeled away his black socks revealing long feet with calloused toes. She ran her hands up his trousered legs, then leaned forward to kiss him.

His hands slid down her spine, cupped her satin-clad butt and toppled her onto him. His mouth muffled her squeal of surprise and she burrowed against him, the rough hair on his chest scrunching against her silky bra, the wool slacks scratching against her legs. She eased her shoes off and let them fall to the floor. Her hands moved eagerly to his waist, but he was there before her, and tugged the trousers off until they too ended on the floor.

Now that he'd made up his mind to stay, he moved against her with a sureness of purpose that took her breath away. His tongue made glorious love to her mouth while his hands molded her body.

He raised his head to watch the movement of the silk

bra against her breasts, and, panting, Jane followed his gaze. Her aching nipples were distended, demanding attention. He stroked the peaks with his fingers until she whimpered, then he followed the same path with his mouth, sucking and pulling until the satin was wet and wrinkled. He blew against the wet spots and she shuddered.

He threw her a wicked grin. "Cold? Better get you out of these wet things."

Reaching behind her he unhooked the lacy excuse for a bra and slipped if off her. Then his mouth came back to her naked breasts while his hand trailed over her belly and stroked her through her silk panties.

Little panting sobs were coming from her throat. Where was her cool detachment? The frank boredom she'd often experienced during sex? "Please," she whispered as her excitement mounted. "You're killing me."

With a satisfied growl he rose up on his knees and stripped off the wisp of silk. His own cotton boxer shorts followed.

She had a quick glimpse of the long hardness of him and then he was pressed up against her, kissing her deeply.

Her hands were eager, restless, dragging down his spine, up his back through his hair and down his back again until she couldn't help tugging his buttocks toward her. She needed him inside her so much she was melting from her own heat.

He resisted her pulling hands. "Not so fast. I want to make this last forever."

He leaned over her and tore one of the packages free.

Once he'd sheathed himself, he lay back down beside her. His hand moved between her thighs and she parted them eagerly. He touched her and she cried out, then he began rubbing in a slow circle. He kissed her once more and his tongue imitated the movement of his fingers, circling the tip of her tongue as though it were a second clit.

The combined sensations drove her half crazy. She was climbing, up and up, and she couldn't hold on much longer. "Please, Spencer I—"

As she caught her breath on a gasp he moved between her legs. She fell on her back and felt him enter her, slow and sure, stretching and filling her until she thought she could bear no more.

Then he moved, and she moved with him, desperate for release. They were both too close to the edge for leisure, and if he'd thought this first time could last anywhere near forever, he was seriously fooling himself. She thrust her hips up to meet him and felt his boiling need, watched the dark concentration on his face. He was holding on, but only barely.

Again and again he plunged, driving her higher and higher until she lost control and began to spin, spiraling through fireworks. She felt the final burst as he groaned aloud and exploded inside her.

16

SPENCER AWOKE with a smile on his face, his right hand curled around the warm globe of Jane's breast, feeling at peace for the first time in months. He resisted waking fully, wanting to drift back into the incredibly erotic dream that seemed to have lasted all night.

A soft sigh came from somewhere nearby. The breast moved and a nipple tickled his palm. He opened his eyes and remembered.

It was no dream. More like a fantasy come to life. Three empty condom packets littered the night table. Spencer felt as if he'd just completed a triathlon.

And won the gold medal.

He took in the golden hair spilled on the pillow beside him. He'd missed a pin, he noted, and leaned forward to ease it from her hair. He remembered taking them out earlier, one by one, just as he had in his fantasies. He'd made her sit naked in front of him while he eased each pin out and a little more gold silk slithered to freedom. Then when her hair was bouncing in wild disarray round her shoulders...

He felt a stirring in his groin just remembering. He felt like a teenager, experiencing sex for the first time. He seemed to have a teenager's insatiable appetites, too. It was faintly embarrassing. Jane hadn't complained though.

He thought about waking her up with his tongue, but squinted at the clock and found it was almost time to get up. He eased up on one elbow just for the pleasure of watching her sleep. Her left hand was flung out and he gazed at it, reliving the moment when she'd pulled off her wedding ring.

That was the moment it had hit him.

He loved her.

He wished she'd been completely honest with him, though. When she drew off the ring, she'd as good as declared that she was available to him. But he'd been so sure she'd tell him the truth—that she'd been single all along. Why hadn't she?

He felt as though he couldn't get enough air into his lungs. Swiftly, careful not to wake her, he slid out of bed and slipped into his clothes. He crept to the desk, found the hotel stationery and pen and wrote Meet me for breakfast—7:30. He hesitated about how to sign off and simply scrawled his initials. If she hadn't figured out last night how he felt about her, no hotel notepad was going to do the job.

Back in his room, he stood under a hot shower for a long time, staring at the slick white tiles through a cloud of steam, letting the jets of hot water pummel him as a niggle of doubt intruded on his post-sex delirium. Why had Jane fixed one lie with a second lie?

Was she buying herself some time?

While he toweled himself dry, he wondered how long it would take before Jane was ready to marry him. He was ready. He wanted to marry her today. God, he loved that woman, and this time he'd be a good husband. He smiled to himself as he imagined being married to Jane.

It might be him nagging her to leave the office earlier.

Considering he'd had no more than a couple of hours' sleep—and he wouldn't have managed that if Jane had traveled with a heftier stash of prophylactics—he felt clear-headed and full of energy. He shaved with extra care. He even blow-dried his hair. While he tried to balance the dryer and, at the same time, brush some semblance of order into the damp mass, he thought about how much he was looking forward to sharing breakfast with Jane and reliving their moment of triumph at Marsden Holt. Hell, he was looking forward to sharing their lives together.

He was whistling as he entered the coffee shop at 7:25. Savoring his first cup of coffee he watched the doorway feeling all eager and slobbery like a puppy watching for its master. He smiled when he looked at his watch ten minutes later. He must really have tired Jane out. She was never late.

It was 7:45 when she finally slid into the chair opposite him.

One look at her face and the sexy nonsense he'd been about to spout dried up. She looked pale, her forehead puckered in a frown. And she wouldn't meet his eyes.

"Did I hurt you?" He said the first thing that came into his head. The night had been so gloriously wild, maybe he'd let himself get carried away. If he'd done something to hurt her, he'd never forgive himself.

The pale cheeks flushed scarlet and she darted a

glance around, presumably to check if he'd been over-heard. "No. No, of course you didn't hurt me."

A deep foreboding settled in his chest. "What's wrong?"

A waiter stopped to fill her coffee cup and Spencer fumed with impatience as she took the time to put milk and sugar in her coffee, stir it and take a slow sip. She held the cup in both hands as though taking comfort from the warmth. Still she wouldn't look at him.

"I can't believe I did such a stupid thing," she finally blurted.

"Stupid?" He practically shouted the word, causing a sudden flurry of interest as bored breakfast eaters turned from their morning papers or business discussions to stare at Spencer, and then at his flushed companion.

He dropped his voice to a fierce whisper. "There are a lot of adjectives I'd use to describe last night. *Fantastic, wild, earth-shattering* come to mind. But *stupid?* What was so stupid about it?"

She looked him in the eye finally, and the anger he read there puzzled him. Now he was wondering if he was the one who'd been stupid. Maybe Jane Stanford liked her fictitious husband just fine. Maybe she had no intention of asking her pretend husband for a pretend divorce. Had he just been her latest conquest? Was the hubster nothing but a cheap excuse not to get serious?

"You sign my paycheck, Spencer."

He blinked at her. "What are you talking about? We have electronic banking. Hal signs your paychecks."

She looked momentarily disconcerted. "Hal?"

"The computer from *2001: A Space Odyssey*. Forget it."

She massaged her temples as though she had a headache. He caught the glint of gold on the fourth finger of her left hand and his heart sank. "You're my boss, Spencer. What kind of woman sleeps with her boss?"

He hardly heard her words. She'd put her wedding ring back on. He got her message loud and clear. "Your wedding ring's back on. What kind of game are you playing?"

"Are you even listening to me? What am I supposed to do? If I take off my wedding ring, everyone will know."

"Everyone will know what?" His voice was dangerously quiet.

"That I slept with my boss."

"Not that there was a lot of sleeping going on. I'd appreciate it if you'd try and remember my name. It's Spencer Tate. I'm a man, not a boss."

"Actually, Spencer, you're both. I finally realized this morning that I can't have one without the other."

His curse was pithy and to the point. It had taken him two years to get over one woman's betrayal, only to make a fool of himself a second time. "Nobody gets everything they want."

"I can't have sex with the man who has the power to fire me."

Anger flowed like molten lava through his body. He shot Jane a look that should have fried her on the spot. She thought he was that kind of a lowlife? Fine. He'd been nice, he'd been patient, he'd been understanding and he'd waited for her to come to him. Now that he'd made love to her and she was trying to reject him, he was all out of patience. "Don't worry," he said as brutally as he could. "You won't get fired. After your performance last night, darling, you deserve a promotion."

He rose from the table, ignoring her strangled gasp and threw his unused napkin on the table. "I'm not hungry. Meet me in the lobby at eight-thirty."

He stalked out of the restaurant wishing he had time to go to the gym. He wanted to punish something. Preferably his own foolish body.

His rage hadn't cooled when they met up again. The lobby was hopping with business people checking in and out and luggage racks spinning back and forth between the front door and the elevators. It was all just a vague background for the woman who stood before him as cold and perfect as a diamond. And as hard.

As much as he wanted to fall on his knees at her feet and beg, to kiss her pale lips until they were pink and swollen with passion, to force her to admit there was a lot more going on between them than a cheap one-night stand, now was not the time. They had a business meeting to attend. This was supposed to be their triumph. He felt as though it was the moment of his most bitter failure.

Someone jostled him from behind, pushing him closer to Jane, perfect in an ice-blue suit. She was right about one thing: he was her boss. He couldn't order her to love him, but he could remind her to act like a professional.

"Jane..." His authoritarian lecture died on the pulpit when she looked at him and he saw the hurt and confusion. In a moment of insight, he realized that the cold exterior was just a shield. She was as mixed-up inside as he was. "Jane..." He tried again. This time her name was a husky appeal. He touched her cheek with his forefinger.

She stepped back, her body telegraphing alarm. Her eyes were looking beyond him again, the rosy color receding.

He had to get her back. He raised his voice so she'd be certain to hear him over the din. "Last night really meant something to me. It wasn't just about sex—"

Her hand jerked up, cutting him off in midsentence. He followed the direction of her horrified gaze and turned to look behind him.

Phil Johnson was staring at Jane as though she were a street hooker. "So, you don't put out for a mere sales manager, but you'll put out for the big boss. Quite a day you had yesterday, scoring Marsden Holt and scori—"

It was pure instinct that brought Spencer's fist forward and shoved it in the ugly sneering mouth. Johnson's attaché case flew one way and his body headed another. He staggered back a few feet and his legs caught on the rim of the lobby fountain.

He swayed back and forth as though undecided whether to regain his feet or plunge into the gurgling water behind him.

Jane stepped forward and made up his mind for him. With a hand on his chest she gave him a shove that toppled him into the water.

Spencer waited for a moment, fists raised, but the man just sat there, water pouring down his head and mixing with the blood dribbling down his chin. He showed no signs of getting up to return the favor.

Spence recalled the story suddenly of Jane punching the same man's lights out and turned to her, knowing how she felt about control. "Hope I didn't steal your thunder. Did you want to take a swing at him?"

She touched his shoulder lightly and smiled at him, the warmest she'd been to him since last night. "I wouldn't want to spoil my manicure." The touch turned to a grip. "You did fine," she said softly, and he had a feeling there was a lot of meaning packed into those three words. He needed to know and damn the consequences. If they were late for the presentation, they were late. Some things were more important than business. "What exactly did you—"

Spencer was interrupted by a strong hand on his arm, and he looked into the beefy face of a hotel security guard. "Would you come this way, sir?" The polite request was belied by the grip of steel on his upper arm.

Johnson was being helped out of the fountain by a second security guard, and Spencer could hear him yelling, "Arrest that man. He assaulted me. Somebody call the cops." He wiped his mouth and gestured to the gathering crowd surrounding the fountain. "Somebody get the names of these witnesses."

Spencer suspected threats of lawsuits wouldn't be far behind. With a sigh he realized he was going to be late for his meeting.

"Listen Jane, this may take a few minutes to straighten out. Take a cab to Marsden Holt. I'll join you as soon as I can."

She glanced at him and at the stocky wrestler type who was ushering him, none too gently, toward a discreet side door off the cavernous lobby. "Don't you want me to stay and explain?"

"No. We've worked too hard for this deal not to see it to the end. Johnson will make as much trouble as he can, but I won't let him spoil our big day. I'll be there if I can, but if not, make some excuse. Go ahead without me. I'm sorry." If he hadn't been so busy talking about their sex life when he should have been keeping his mind on business, it wouldn't have happened.

"I'm sorry," he said again, louder, as the guard led him away. He wanted to kiss her, just to bring some more color back to her cheeks. He wasn't a violent man, but he also wanted another half hour or so with Mr. Johnson in an alley somewhere that didn't contain hired security guards.

Jane nodded, glanced at her watch, and with a little shake, seemed to pull herself together. She pulled out a business card and ran up to hand it to the security guard. "I can't miss this meeting, but I hope you'll phone me on my cell so I can explain what happened."

"It's not up to me, ma'am. I'll give your card to our head of security."

Jane nodded, sent Spencer one last concerned glance and walked slowly out of the hotel. As she did, she turned more heads than a movie star. And, for once, Spencer didn't think it was just her undeniable beauty causing the craning necks.

He wanted to call out to her, explain that his comment in the restaurant had been a defensive reaction. Of course, he didn't feel that way, but she was walking out the door with that straight spine at odds with the sweet swing of her hips. And she didn't look back.

TWICE JANE opened her lips to tell the cab driver to turn around. She wanted to be there for Spencer. She wanted to thank him for doing the Johnson job properly, to make sure Johnson didn't end up twisting the story.

She knew it was stupid of Spence to have hauled off and clobbered Johnson, but damn, it had felt good watching him. It was comforting, somehow, to know she wasn't the only person in the world who wanted to smack the sexist leer off Phil Johnson's face.

But Spencer's expression as the muscle-bound security officer had hauled him away hadn't been one of satisfaction. He'd looked haunted.

Never had she felt less businesslike or less professional. She'd broken her own cardinal rule and already paid a huge price. Her professional reputation was ruined—Johnson would make sure of that. If only Spencer had kept his mouth shut. If only she hadn't broken her own rule.

And what of Spencer? What would he think of her now? When they were in meetings together would he be listening to her ideas as a professional sales person or indulging her whims as his mistress? She dropped her head into her hand. *Mistress* was a term her mother would use, but as modern as Jane considered herself, she'd still done an incredibly stupid thing.

Well, this was no time to fall to pieces. She had to represent Datatracker for both herself and Spencer, and she'd do a great job if it killed her.

The cab rumbled through the gray morning while she marshaled her emotions. Closing her eyes, she drew a few slow, deep breaths and tried to visualize a successful presentation. It wasn't even a presentation, only a short speech. Or was it? Until now she'd assumed Spencer would do most of the talking, and she'd simply say a few words. But would he even make the meeting? He didn't know Johnson the way she did.

The man was quite capable of lying to save his skin—and even more likely to twist the truth if there was any chance at all of causing Spencer to look bad in the eyes of Marsden Holt.

Jane had to accept the possibility that she'd be making the Thank-you-for-your-confidence-we-won't-let-you-down speech alone. Visualization was a technique that usually worked for her, but today the only vision she could drag up was that of Spencer's face as he was being dragged away from her. He'd looked as if he'd been the one beaten.

The cab drew up in front of Marsden Holt long before she'd approached the zenlike calm for which she'd been striving. She pasted a phony smile on her face and walked through the double glass doors and into the football-field-sized atrium that served as the company's reception area. A pleasant blond woman approached and upon finding out who she was, gestured Jane to a chair while she returned to her work area and picked up the phone.

The atrium was cool, full of some kind of textured stone tile, glass walls and leafy dark-green plants. But for all the serenity it suggested, Jane was deeply aware of the hum of energy throughout the building. Curving staircases rose from each side to an open second level. Looking up she watched workers come and go, or huddle in whispering groups. It struck her as odd that the men all wore suits, and she didn't hear any laughter. She'd become accustomed to Datatracker's casual atmosphere.

Her reverie was interrupted by a smiling John Marsden, coming down one of the staircases toward her. She rose with an answering smile and extended her hand.

"Jane," he said, beaming, "this is a very exciting day." He looked around expectantly and then raised his brows in a silent question.

Keeping the smile in place, Jane said, "Spencer sends his apologies. An emergency's come up. He'll try to make it for a few minutes if he can, but I think we should go ahead without him."

"I'm happy to have you to myself for a bit," he said.

She attached her security pass to her lapel, and, squaring her shoulders, turned to John Marsden trying her best to look in control—of what, she wasn't quite sure.

"Did you see the gong?" he asked her.

"It's pretty hard to miss." The gong was a huge brass disk about the size of a satellite dish with a muscular-looking hammer suspended beneath it.

"We bang it when we have a big announcement to make." He shrugged, "It's an idea left over from a Japanese management-style book that impressed my partner Evan Holt back in the eighties." Since she knew that Mr. Holt was a major financial partner who was hardly ever seen, she merely smiled.

As she accompanied the company president to his office, she noticed again how formal everyone seemed. John Marsden had a pleasant hello for everyone he passed, but the responses were respectful and polite. She couldn't help comparing the atmosphere with the energetic, irreverent give-and-take one at Datatracker.

Six months ago, if she'd been asked which kind of atmosphere she'd prefer to work in, Jane wouldn't have hesitated to choose the more formal company. Now she knew she loved creative chaos and high energy.

But thinking of Datatracker made her think of Spencer and that was a bad idea if she hoped to get through this day. Part of her mind was obsessed with what was happening to him. Should she have stayed to make it clear he was defending her when he attacked Johnson?

"Jane?"

"Hmm?" She came back to her surroundings with a jolt at the quiet question.

"I was asking whether you prefer a cappuccino or a plain coffee."

"I'm sorry, John. Plain coffee's fine, thanks."

He picked up the phone and ordered coffees. They made small talk while waiting. John Marsden sat in a leather chair behind a heavy mahogany desk. She perched across from him in a leather visitor's chair.

As soon as the coffee had been delivered by an elegant assistant and they had busied themselves with cream and sugar, John Marsden leaned back and said, "Well, Jane. I promised Spencer I wouldn't try to steal you, and I'm a man of my word, so I'll just say that Datatracker is very lucky to have you." He paused. "I've been looking for someone to groom as VP of Sales for ages, with no luck." He smiled at her and took a sip of his coffee.

What to say? Jane felt hot and cold all at once. She hadn't had to bring up the subject—she was being offered a chance to hint that she'd love to work for Marsden Holt. It was her chance to get away from the complicated relationship with Spencer, to distance herself from whatever slime Johnson planned to sling her way, and to work for a terrific company. She should be jumping up and down. Instead, words were sticking in her throat.

"I...um...that's very nice of you to say."

"You're a talented young woman. I hope you'll stay in touch."

"Of course." So why wasn't she crawling under the desk to kiss Mr. Marsden's Florsheim-clad feet instead of feeling this hollow ache in her chest?

He reached into his wallet and removed a business card which he handed to Jane.

"I already have your card."

"This one has my home number as well. Just in case."

Jane laughed. She couldn't help it. The sly old fox. "Thank you for a wonderful compliment. I'll keep it in mind."

With a glance at his watch, John Marsden said, "We've planned the announcement for eleven. Would you like to tour the operation while we're waiting?"

She'd already toured the plant twice. A surreptitious

glance at her own watch told her they had thirty minutes until the announcement. "That would be great," she lied. "But first, could I visit the ladies' room?"

"Of course." He rose courteously and escorted her to the door. "I'll meet you back at the front desk."

After checking that the ladies' room was deserted, Jane hauled out her cell phone. She'd turned her phone off while she'd been with John Marsden, and in that short time, someone had left a message. With a sinking heart, she retrieved it and, as she'd dreaded, it was Spence sounding clipped and frustrated telling her he wouldn't be able to make it.

She tried to reach him but in turn got his recorded message. Obviously, Johnson was making threats and dragging this thing out for all it was worth. For a moment she was tempted to make her excuses and head straight back to the hotel. It wasn't fair that Spence should suffer for what he'd done...

She caught a glimpse of herself in the mirror. *Is this the reflection of a woman who's VP material? Pull yourself together!* Spencer wouldn't want her running to his side as his lover; he'd want her to do her job. So she had to take part in the big announcement on her own. Big deal. So what if her whole life was a shambles? She was a professional and she would act like one.

Grimly she pulled out her toiletry bag and retouched the concealer that was doing a lousy job of hiding the black circles under her eyes. She fixed her lipstick, tucked a few stray tendrils back in her chignon, and tried to put some color into her pale cheeks with blusher. Even after all her efforts, she still looked pale. "Well," she informed her reflection, "it's show-time. Let's go bang a gong—and pretend it's Johnson's face."

17

SPENCER was not a happy man.

By the time he was able to leave, he'd missed not only the Marsden Holt event but also the plane Jane was on. He had to take a later flight and he also had to contend with his own thoughts and memories. In the space of twenty-four hours, he'd climbed an emotional Everest then plummeted to the floor of the Grand Canyon.

By the time he was home, he was at least calmer, but he didn't remember the last time he'd been so messed up emotionally. His bruised knuckles were a constant reminder that playing Spencer the Avenger had pretty much blown up in his face.

Johnson had done his best to press charges. Spencer had a feeling two things had saved his butt on that front. First, both men were from out of the country and second an older couple had knocked politely on the security chief's door and offered themselves as witnesses to the exchange. Spencer's heart had sunk when he'd first seen them. They looked like Mr. and Mrs. Bush, senior. Who could doubt the word of a woman who looked like a kindly grandmother and former first lady? They'd probably seen him punch Johnson without any clue as to why. With Barbara against him, he'd probably get the death penalty. But, as it turned out, the older couple was here to corroborate his story.

Luckily for him, they'd overheard Johnson's provoking comments as well as seen Spencer's fist fly.

"It's nice to see a young man with an old-fashioned sense of chivalry," said the Barbara Bush clone, patting his shoulder kindly. Spencer, even in his deep gratitude, was awfully glad Jane hadn't been around to hear those words.

It was late Friday night when he finally reached home. He called Jane's home and her cell, cursing when he got nothing but voice mail. He was bitterly disappointed that he couldn't talk to her, although he didn't have a clue what he could say or do that would prove to that stubborn, misguided woman that he was honest-to-God in love with her and that it wouldn't impede their business relationship.

He checked his own messages and discovered three from Chelsea. By the third message her voice didn't sound all that calm. He almost groaned. He hadn't liked the misery in her voice when she'd told him that things weren't exactly hunky-dory with her and his brother. What could he do or say to help? She was a trained psychologist and didn't seem to be doing such a hot job fixing her own problems. How could he—a divorced man who'd just done his best to screw up his latest relationship—possibly advise her?

He sighed. She was always there for him. He could at least let her vent, or cry on his shoulder. And he could keep his own problems out of the conversation.

He allowed himself the luxury of a shower, then

poured himself a well-deserved Scotch, sank to his favorite chair and called Chelsea.

"Oh, thank goodness you called. I was getting desperate." She sounded to him as though she was already there.

"I was out of town. What's up?"

"I need you to water my plants and feed the fish for a couple of weeks. Can you do that?"

He shook his head in disbelief. "Yeah. Of course. Where are you going?"

"I took your advice. I'm going to Africa."

"What?" The ice cubes clinked against his glass as he plonked it on the table.

"You were right, Spencer. No marriage—heck, no relationship—works without compromise. I talked to Bill on the phone finally and I'm going out for a couple of weeks. He'll take some time off and we'll figure out a way to make this thing work. He can go on fewer digs. Maybe I can change my teaching schedule so I can join him more often. The point is, we love each other too much to screw up this marriage."

Spencer felt a warm glow in his chest that had nothing to do with the fact that it was his most excellent advice that had helped his brother and Chelsea sort out their problems.

Once he was off the phone, the glow grew into a lightning bolt of inspiration.

Of course, the answer was staring at him. If Chelsea and Bill, two of the most stubborn people he knew, could find a way to compromise and mesh their professional and personal lives, then so could he and Jane.

So long as she loved him as much as he loved her, they could do anything.

It was a big if, though. She hadn't said she loved him, hadn't even come clean about her lie. However, after the performance Johnson had put on, he had a considerably better understanding of why Jane had undertaken her crazy scheme.

But all lies were off tomorrow. He and Jane were going to have a very long heart-to-heart, and he wasn't planning on leaving until she admitted the truth.

"MY GOSH, you already look pregnant!" were the first words out of Jane's mouth when Alicia and Chuck dropped by her apartment the next morning with fresh croissants. She knew her best friend couldn't be more than about four months along.

She was still groggy from arriving late last night and having yet another lousy sleep. She wore sweats and no makeup and had barely managed to brush her hair and teeth before her friends arrived.

"Thanks," Alicia said, gazing down at her own protruding belly. "My ego really needed a boost."

"Sorry, I meant you look...um...pregnant, but good." She'd never seen a woman go from just-found-out to maternity clothes so fast.

Alicia's bulging belly wobbled with her laughter. "It's twins. Can you believe it? Chuck nearly had a fit when he found out he has to buy two of everything. But he cheered up when I told him he only has to buy me flowers once."

"Aw, honey," Chuck said, laying a hand over his wife's round stomach, "I think it's great." He hovered around like a mother hen, fussing and cooing, making sure Alicia sat on the couch with her feet raised and a cushion behind her back. He even elbowed Jane out of the kitchen to prepare decaffeinated coffee.

Amused, and rather touched, Jane sat across from Alicia and enjoyed the spectacle of Chuck pampering his pregnant wife.

While he made coffee, Alicia said, "Pass me a croissant, will you Jane? I feel like an insatiable alien has taken over my body. I spend my whole day either looking for food or a bathroom."

With a chuckle, Jane fetched the bag, which was surprisingly heavy and one peek inside told her why. "Alicia, there are at least three dozen croissants in here."

"Is that all? You better not have one then."

"Don't be greedy, honey. I can get some more if we run out," the usually tight-fisted Chuck said, causing both women to stare at each other in shock.

"I should have let him knock me up years ago," Alicia mumbled through her croissant.

Chuck brought the coffee over and squeezed himself in behind Alicia so her head was resting on his chest. He put a proprietary hand on her belly and sighed with what could only be fatherly pride.

Jane couldn't have been more happy that Chuck and Alicia had dropped by this morning. Alone, she'd only have brooded some more. As though she hadn't done enough of that all night.

"So do you have names picked out yet?" Jane snuggled back into her chair and curled her feet under her. It was so good to have friends to take her mind off her problems with Spencer, even if they also filled her with yearning for that kind of closeness, that kind of family.

"Well, if it's a girl, we're thinking of—"

The sound of knocking on the door caught her in mid-sentence.

Rising, Jane excused herself. "It's probably my neighbor—she collects my newspaper when I'm away," she mumbled over a large bite of croissant she'd just taken.

But it wasn't Mrs. Rosenbaum. The sight in front of her made her choke and splutter. "Spencer!"

"I'm sorry to barge in on you like this, Jane. But I have to talk to you. Somebody downstairs let me in."

The shock of seeing him made a chunk of bread go down the wrong way. She couldn't manage to speak, only to wave her arms around like a maniac.

He smirked. "What's the matter, is your husband here?"

Shaking her head wildly while coughing brought tears to her eyes.

Spencer looked at her with concern. "You need a glass of water."

"Is everything all right, Jane?" Chuck called out.

"Uh-uh," she choked out.

She was so busy trying to get her breath back that she forgot to stop Spencer on his journey down the hall, and suddenly they were in the living room where she piled into Spencer who'd stopped dead.

"Morning Alicia, Chuck."

She racked her sluggish brain, but the sight confronting Spencer was pretty tough to explain. Chuck was on his knees in front of Alicia kissing her swollen belly.

He raised his head, and, seeing Spencer, blushed and stumbled awkwardly to his feet.

"Don't get up on my account," Spencer said pleasantly.

It was like a still photograph. Everyone seemed frozen in place. Alicia had a welcoming smile glued to her lips, along with half a dozen flaky croissant crumbs. Chuck had the foolish look of a man caught cooing over his unborn child, and Spencer looked like a man trying to decide whether to laugh or start yelling.

He glanced Jane's way, but she was as rooted to the spot as the rest of them.

He was the first to break the tableau, stepping into the living room and addressing Alicia, with a glance at her rounded belly. "I see congratulations are in order."

Chuck pulled himself up to his full height and glared at Jane with an I-told-you-this-would-never-work expression. He swallowed, his Adam's apple bobbing. "Would you care to step outside? I think we should talk. Man to man."

"Not particularly. It looks like rain," Spencer said, still as pleasant. "Is that coffee?"

"Thanks. It's twins. And the coffee's decaf," Alicia said, her voice slightly muffled by croissant.

"Uh, Spencer," Jane said. "It's, uh...not what you think."

"Croissant?" Alicia pushed the bag at Spencer.

"Thanks, Alicia," he said, and took his time choosing one.

Chuck, loyal friend that he was, rose, crossed to Jane and put his arm around her. "Darling," he said, "isn't it great that Alicia and her husband are having a baby?"

"Maybe you and Jane should think about a family," Spencer said affably, the maddening twinkle in his espresso eyes becoming more pronounced. He broke off a piece of croissant and popped it in his mouth, but not before Jane had seen his grin. Why, he didn't even seem very surprised. Her eyes narrowed.

Alicia's lips quivered.

Chuck scratched his head. "I...uh, that's something to think about, isn't it Jane?"

Jane was glad to have Chuck's arm around her. She needed the support.

"I told Jane it was the craziest idea I'd ever heard," Alicia told Spencer.

"Sure was." He spoke to Alicia as though he'd dropped by specially to see and talk to her. "I saw the two of you at Il Paradiso a few weeks back. At first, I thought Chuck was having an affair with his wife's best friend."

That was too much for Chuck to take. Pushing his glasses up his nose, he stepped forward. "I love Alicia. I'd never cheat on her. No offense, Jane."

"None taken," she said faintly.

"Aw, honey," Alicia's voice was thick with sudden tears. She stood awkwardly and pulled Chuck to her. "He may not be Tom Cruise," she said to Jane, "but I love him." And she took his face in her hands and kissed him soundly. "And now, I think it's time we left. Jane needs to talk to Spencer."

Jane shot a glance at Spencer, who had clearly figured out who was married to whom, and quailed. "No really, Alicia. Don't go. You haven't finished your breakfast."

"Goodbye Alicia! Look after her, Chuck," Spencer said in a tone that brooked no refusal.

"Um. Do you think it's wise to leave Jane alone with him?" Chuck asked his wife in a stage whisper.

Alicia harrumphed. "Wisdom never had much to do with this mess. But it's Jane's mess. Let her sort it out her way."

Jane felt the blood draining from her head and sat down before she fainted.

From a great distance it seemed she heard Alicia say, "Don't be too hard on her. She can't help being screwed up." And in a louder voice, "I'll call you later, Jane. Um...Do you mind if I take the rest of the croissants?"

"No," she croaked.

With a rustle of paper bag and a flurry of whispers, Chuck and Alicia left and the apartment seemed suddenly too small.

Silence. Thick, unbroken silence. When she couldn't stand it another second, she said, "You've known since—"

"Since I spotted Chuck and Alicia having an anniversary dinner." He sipped his coffee and she twiddled with her stupid fake ring while seconds ticked by.

She couldn't think of a single thing to say.

"Have you ever been married?" Spencer asked.

Around and around went the bright gold wedding ring, transfixing her so that she was unable to lift her eyes. "No."

"I thought you'd tell me. I waited, tried everything I could think of to force you to admit the truth."

"What truth? That I'm single? Okay. I'm single."

"No. The truth that something was happening between us. You kept hiding behind a phony ring and a phony marriage."

She felt a prick of tears which infuriated her. She never cried. "I didn't mean for any of this to happen."

"What about me falling in love with you? Did you mean that to happen?"

He loved her. She'd fooled herself thinking they could have a quiet, discreet affair. He wasn't that kind of man. And she didn't think she was that kind of woman. His tone wasn't soft and loving, though. He sounded pretty damned irritated, which was basically the same way she felt.

"Stop making a federal case out of it. I stuck a wedding ring on my finger to protect myself from jerks like Johnson."

"And from me?"

She couldn't stand him stooping over her like some avenging angel. She shot up out of her chair and stepped toward him. "Yes, and you. You're my boss. You know what they say about women who sleep with the boss? There are lots of cute expressions—*the casting couch, dipping your pen in the company ink*—"

"You let me think you were a married woman when you knew I was falling for you."

"I threw away my career for you!"

"Your career. That's all that matters to you. News flash—you're terrific at what you do. You could get a job anywhere, selling anything. But finding someone you click with, well that doesn't happen every day."

One part of his rant came through loud and clear. She could get a job anywhere. Obviously, he'd come to the same conclusion she had. They couldn't conduct an affair and work together. Still, he could have at least offered to be the one to leave. He'd been as much a party to their night of passion as she had. But, as she'd known all along, when it came down to the wire, she was the one who'd be leaving Datatracker, not the CEO. "Don't worry," she told him. "I am looking for another job."

He looked as though she'd smacked him a good one. "I hope it can keep you warm on winter nights. I thought we had a future." With that he turned on his heels and stalked down the hall and out of her apartment.

She sat there, stunned. What was he so huffy about? Wasn't she giving him exactly what he wanted? She'd get another job. They could carry on an affair, long distance, if necessary. It was the only chance they had.

Wasn't it?

She sat for a long time curled in the chair. At last she tugged the ring off her finger and threw it across the room. It bounced off the pale lavender wall and plopped to the floor.

He'd thrown the words at her like an insult, but she had felt the truth. She sniffed. A man she didn't believe she'd ever find—a man she could love and respect— had all but told her he loved her. And she'd thrown her chance of happiness away because of a stupid lie.

One tear rolled down her cheek. She brushed it away. Crying was for wimps.

A second tear followed, and then the whole Hoover Dam burst in a great racking sob.

A long time and two boxes of tissues later, she dug out John Marsden's business card.

18

MONDAY dawned.

Jane was absolutely, one hundred percent certain it dawned because she was awake to see it. She had been awake all night in fact, composing, printing and tearing up resignation letters, each one less satisfactory than the one before.

Damn it, she couldn't even get past the salutation. Dear Spencer was too personal, Dear Mr. Tate hypocritical. After all, the man had been inside her body. She supposed they were on a first-name basis. Which is what made the letter impossible to write. How could she be truthful?

How would the truth even read? She began typing.

Dear Spencer:
Having had intimate sexual relations with you, I no longer feel you will treat me as a professional.

And there she stopped. The blinking cursor urged her on, but something soft and squishy was happening deep in her belly when it occurred to her that that was another lie.

She knew instinctively that he would treat her as a professional as long as she acted like one. Outside of office hours she could be his lover and act as crazily as she wanted, but once she stepped into her business suit she knew he'd stop being her lover and be her colleague.

She was enough of an adult and a professional to conduct two different relationships with the same person. Why, she and Alicia had worked together by day and been best friends by night for several years, acting totally differently at the office than they did after business hours. There'd been no conflict. She had to believe Spencer could be just as professional. And she found that she did believe it.

With a quaking sense of shame, she deleted that sentence and started the letter again.

Dear Spencer:
Having lied about my marital status on my application for employment with your company, and during my tenure as Sales Manager, I no longer feel...

What? What did she no longer feel? She'd done what she'd done for a good reason at the time. How could she possibly have known she'd meet the man of her dreams at Datatracker?

But it was a waste of time wishing she could change the past. She couldn't. She could only try and rectify the damage and move forward. Living with the pain of losing Spencer was ample punishment for her stupidity.

Coward that she was, she considered not showing up for work and simply sending her resignation by courier. But she couldn't do that. Spencer deserved at least the courtesy of receiving her resignation letter from her in person, and perhaps, if he felt inclined to listen to anything she had to say, an explanation for her behavior.

No doubt the resignation letter would end up in her personnel file. Spencer's eyes would not be the only ones to read whatever she wrote.

Dawn bloomed into early morning as she typed the final draft of the letter, which ended her career of lies at Datatracker with one more lie. She claimed that she was leaving because of a job offer elsewhere, and spouted a load of the usual insincere platitudes. If she'd had more time she could have spent hours more writing and rewriting. But she didn't. So she printed the thing on the cream vellum personal stationary her parents had given her one Christmas, signed it with swift strokes and a sinking heart and readied herself for the office with shaking hands and a hollow belly.

Once she got to the office she didn't even try to avoid him. Instead, she headed straight for his office.

"Hi, Yumi," she greeted his assistant with a nervous smile.

The other woman sent her a distracted glance. "If you want Spencer, you'll have to join the line. He's got meetings 'till noon, then—"

Jane didn't hear another word. Spencer was standing in his doorway looking at her with such an array of emotions on his face she couldn't have said which was dominant. Anger? Hurt? Bewilderment? Sadness? Love?

He looked endearingly rumpled. His hair was a mess, his eyes were red-rimmed and from the patch of toilet paper sticking to his chin, she guessed he'd cut himself shaving.

Swallowing was painful. Her mouth was suddenly as dry as the desert.

"Jane. Come in." It sounded kind of croaky—maybe he had a dry mouth too. For some reason the thought gave her courage.

"But Spencer—" Yumi said sharply, then, looking from one to the other, she shook her head and picked up the phone. "I'll start rearranging. You've got a half hour, tops."

Walking into his office for the last time made Jane want to cry. So much for the professional demeanor she'd promised herself. She sank into the gray leather chair she'd occupied on her first visit to this office six months ago, when he'd interviewed her for the job— when she'd worn her shiny new fake wedding band for the first time, still believing she'd never fall in love.

The sound of the office door closing jerked her head up and she turned to face the man she'd fallen in love with. The worst man she could have chosen. Her boss.

Spencer didn't look like either the man she loved or her boss, however. He looked like a stranger, his face a careful mask. He passed by her and, instead of flopping into the matching gray chair as he usually did, he walked around his desk and sat behind it. She wasn't sure whether he did that to remind her he was the boss—as if she needed reminding—or whether he simply wanted to put a physical barrier between them. His action was absurdly hurtful, in any case.

No one spoke. She had a feeling neither of them wanted to open the conversation that would effectively end their relationship—both professional and personal. Plus, in her case, her throat was so dry she didn't think she was capable of speech.

Instead, she drank in the sight of him, knowing it might well be the last time. His eyes were bloodshot and his face had a gray tint to it. His hair was a worse disaster than ever. She wondered when it had last been in contact with a comb. It looked as if he'd used a lawn mower to shave. If she didn't know him better, she'd have said he'd been drinking.

When he raised a hand to rub it over his face her eyes widened. The hand was shaking. He muttered a curse when he felt the toilet paper bandage and he yanked it off, cursing again when it pulled free and the nick began bleeding.

He glanced around helplessly, then shoved a finger up against the bleeding spot. "Do you see any tissues?"

"I doubt Search and Rescue could find anything in your office." Digging in her briefcase she extracted a travel pack of tissues and put it on his desk.

Forcing her gaze away from the somehow intimate action of him staunching a shaving cut she studied his desk instead. An open bottle of painkillers and a large glass of water told their own tale. He *had* been drinking. Probably while she'd been having her crying jag.

Somehow, knowing she'd made him as miserable as he'd made her was reassuring. And it gave her the courage to dig into her briefcase once again, this time for the slim cream envelope containing her resignation letter. She knew it was better to end things quickly and avoid dragging out the pain.

She slipped the envelope onto the desk in front of him.

He studied it for a moment and then, ignoring it, raised his eyes and gazed directly at her. "You look like hell," he said.

There was a lump in her throat she had to swallow before she could answer, "You, too."

Gingerly he pulled the tissue away from his chin and this time the wound stayed closed. He tossed the tissue at the trash can and missed. Then he jutted his chin toward the envelope he still hadn't touched. "Is that what I think it is?"

She nodded. And then, because she was a professional and didn't want any misunderstandings she said, "It's my letter of resignation."

The flash of pain crossed his face so quickly she almost could have imagined it. "You're giving two weeks' notice I hope?"

Why had she ever thought he'd try and make this easy for her?

"I was hoping to leave sooner. As soon as possib— today, actually."

He rubbed his eyes like a man functioning on too little sleep. "But what about Marsden Holt? We could use your help getting set up for the installation. Surely you owe us that."

This wasn't going the way she'd hoped at all. Instead of being glad to be rid of her, he was making her feel like a worm for leaving. Her gaze dropped to the carpet and she forced herself not to squirm.

"I'm thinking of taking a job with Marsden Holt." As hard as she'd tried, thinking was as far as she'd gone.

She'd stared at John Marsden's home number so many times over the weekend that she had it memorized, but she hadn't been able to make the call.

Spencer emitted a crack of laughter that sounded harsh and bitter. Glancing up, she saw that he had risen from behind his desk and was stalking to the window. "John Marsden gave me his word he wouldn't try to steal you. Doesn't anybody tell the goddamn truth anymore?"

Her own lies were indefensible, but she couldn't allow Spencer to feel so betrayed. She forced herself to speak clearly. "He didn't steal me. He simply made it clear they would be interested if I ever—"

"What did he promise you? More money?" The fury she heard in his voice was visible in the reflection of his angry face in the window.

"No. He didn't promise me—"

"A fancier title?"

She flinched, and he must have seen the truth on her face.

Refusing to tell any more lies, even to save his feelings, she admitted the truth. "He gave me his home number at our last meeting, the one you couldn't make, and dropped hints they were looking for someone to groom for the position of VP of Sales."

"I couldn't make that meeting because I was being thrown out of the country for acting like a damn Boy Scout. Giving you the chance to stab me in the back."

"That's not how it happened!" Her voice rose.

"Isn't it?"

"No." She remembered the vile things Phil Johnson had said to her and the rush of feral satisfaction she'd experienced when Spencer sent him flying. "I was very grateful to you for putting Johnson in his place. But afterward I got to thinking that he'll spread that story as fast as his nasty little mouth can move. He'll destroy my credibility and damage yours. I can't let that happen."

"I thought you loved this job. I can't believe you're just walking away."

"I was wrong to lie about being married, Spencer. I realize that now. I want to leave with some dignity and start again somewhere else. I..." She absentmindedly started to fiddle with her fake wedding ring, only to feel herself blush when she realized she wasn't wearing it.

"I got fired from my last job. Johnson...well he acted inappropriately and I lost my temper. That's why I bought the ring and pretended to be married. But he's never forgiven me for rejecting me."

Spencer didn't look a bit surprised, just nodded as she stumbled her way through the story. "I know all that," he said when she'd finished and sat there looking at him, waiting for some indication of surprise or outrage.

"You know? How did you—?"

"I checked up on you before I hired you. You're not dealing with a moron, you know. Well, I'm not usually a moron though I did buy that crock of bull about you being married."

"But—but I can't believe you'd hire me when you found out about Johnson. Did you know I hit him?"

He grinned in that way he had that always made her knees weak. "That's when I decided to hire you."

"Then you must understand that I couldn't stay knowing that he caught us...that he heard you—"

"Johnson is a cockroach. And this isn't about him. It's about you not having any guts."

Jane gasped in shock, her gaze shooting up to lock with his angry storm-cloud eyes. "How dare you! It takes guts to work in a man's world and get ahead. I've put up with sexual harassment, locker-room jokes, I've even had to learn to play golf."

The storm lightened slightly as his eyes twinkled. "That must have hurt."

"The point is, it's a boys' club, and I either play by men's rules or I don't get to play at all."

"You've climbed up so high on that soapbox of yours you can't even see down here to the real world anymore. All that high-and-mighty talk is a convenient cover. You're scared and you're running."

Hands firmly on her hips she glared at him belligerently. "And just what am I scared of?"

"This!" And before she had a chance to move, he had pulled her into his arms for the mother of all tongue-lashings. He lashed her lips, her tongue—all the dark secret places inside her mouth. And pretty soon she gave back as good as she got, getting in some pretty good licks of her own.

She felt herself being manhandled back into the gray leather chair and she whimpered deep in her throat. Her hands buried themselves into his hair.

"This is what you're scared of." His heated words burned her flesh as he trailed kisses from her mouth down her throat.

"I'm not, I... Oh, we shouldn't be doing this, it's inappropriate, I—"

The sharp buzz of the intercom halted both of them.

A gasp of horror escaped Jane's swollen lips.

"Spencer?" Yumi's staticky voice echoed through the room. "Ed Pospett is here."

Frantically, Jane straightened her clothing and grabbed her bag to find her lipstick while Spencer leapt for the intercom. His voice sounded calm enough, maybe a little deeper than normal, as he replied, "We're just wrapping up. I'll be another five minutes."

He might sound calm, Jane thought, but there was a suspicious bulge below his belt that betrayed his state.

Of all people to be on the other side of the door. She couldn't believe her bad luck. Ed Pospett was chairman of the board of directors for Datatracker—an executive of the old school, as starchy and pompous as they'd ever been made.

If she'd been pale before, she knew she was beet-red now and so shaky she could hardly aim the lipstick at the right part of her face. She shoved her briefcase over her shoulder and was scuttling toward the door when Spencer grabbed her arm and stopped her flight.

"This is not over," he whispered. "Your resignation is not accepted."

Her eyes widened and her lips parted in surprise.

He took advantage and kissed her, quick and hard.

"Don't leave town," he ordered.

For a moment Jane contemplated punishing Spencer by letting him meet with the chairman of the board with her lipstick all over his mouth, but at the last moment she gave him a break.

"Wipe your mouth," she tossed back. And as she opened the door to walk out with as much dignity as she could muster, she saw him doing just that, furtively scrubbing pink gloss off his lips with the back of his hand.

19

SCARED? Who was Spencer calling scared?

"I am not scared!" she said sternly, tossing a handful of birdseed like buckshot, effectively scaring the mallards, swans and assorted other birds flapping and floating in Lost Lagoon.

She had been so flustered when she'd left Spencer's office that she'd kept walking right out the door. She'd instinctively headed for her apartment and then realized that this was the last place she wanted to be. Her phone was there, her home fax, her computer and e-mail. She didn't want to be connected to the world, not just yet. She'd quickly changed into jeans and a T-shirt and shoved her feet into socks and sneakers.

Her feet had led her to Stanley Park of their own volition. On the way past a corner store she'd grabbed a bag of wild birdseed. Feeding the birds always brought her a sense of peace.

Traffic hummed behind her, but it was only background noise. The squawking birds with their greedy snapping beaks commanded most of her attention. She tossed as much seed as she could to the perimeter of the quacking feathery vortex for the smaller, more timid creatures. The swans just floated serenely, knowing their beauty and dignity alone would bring them ample seed. She chuckled, liking their attitude.

It felt good to be out in the fresh air, and temporarily away from her troubles, although Spencer's assertion that she was scared had ruffled *her* feathers more than she liked. Was she scared? Scared of the intimacy and commitment that love entailed? Afraid to give up control of any part of her, even her heart, to another?

The thoughts echoed around her head with a kind of truth to them she didn't like.

Loving Spencer was complicated, not impossible. But did she have the courage to love him?

She would have to face the fact that she'd become that which she most scorned, a female employee sleeping with the boss. She'd have to face down gossip and criticism. And that was just at work. Outside of office hours they'd have to forge a personal life that didn't involve the office. That wasn't going to be easy for a couple of workaholics.

Was he worth the effort?

She chuckled as she sprinkled the last of the birdseed. From the way they'd both reacted when she'd tried to resign, she had her answer. Her body had known what her mind had been slower to accept. Damn right he was worth it.

She glanced at her watch, and realized with a shock she'd spent most of the day communing with nature and sorting through her thoughts and feelings. She'd have to hurry if she wanted to catch Spencer before he left work for the day, and before he changed his mind and decided to accept her resignation after all.

She half walked, half jogged home, humming with anticipation, trying to figure out what she was going to say to him. Jane felt irritation sluice through her when she had to pause at her building's entrance while an elderly woman chatted pleasantly to the tall man heading in.

The man put his hand higher up on the doorframe, taking its weight while the older woman smiled at something he said.

He must have heard her keys jangling; he turned his head and she recognized him.

"Spencer!"

"Hi Jane. Come on in."

Her eyebrows rose of their own accord. "This is supposed to be a secure building."

"I have an honest face." He sent her a look that didn't appear honest at all. It was absolutely, deliciously wicked, and his espresso eyes were sending messages straight to the quivering core of her.

"So what do you want?" She asked as, by mutual consent, they both headed for the stairs and skipped the elevator.

He held the heavy metal fire door open for her and they paced up the cement stairs together. "We have unfinished business," he said, his words echoing in the cement stairwell.

And that's a double entendre if I ever heard one, she thought with a secret kind of exultation.

Once she got him inside her apartment, the exultation turned to nervous excitement. It was going to be tough enough to tell him she wanted her job back, but doing it in her apartment was going to be even harder.

She led him automatically into the living room. "Please, sit down." She gestured to a chair, allowing her training in good manners to help her function with some kind of normalcy even though her stomach was doing flips.

After he'd plopped down, with seeming reluctance, on the chair she'd indicated, she sat opposite him on the couch, her knees and ankles pressed neatly together.

There was a tiny pause, and she realized that he was leaving it to her to begin. Jane licked her lips. "Would you care for something to drink?"

"No thanks."

How did she open up the conversation?

"Something to eat, perhaps?"

Amusement tickled his features as he shook his head.

There was another pause as she marshaled her arguments. Her head felt as if it was stuffed with cotton candy. Every time she glanced at him, she felt overcome with heat as memories of the way she'd lost control in his office that morning filled her.

After an eternity of agonizing about what she was going to say, she realized Spencer was looking for something. He patted his pockets, shoved a hand in one tweed crevice after another, and finally, with a small cry of triumph, pulled a creased paper out of his shirt pocket and extended it toward her.

"Is that my resignation?" If it was, it had been badly abused since she had handed it to him that morning crisply folded in a snowy envelope.

He shook his head. "Not yours. Mine."

"What?" She let out a shriek that would have done Alicia proud. "Spencer, are you crazy? You're the president of a terrific company. You'd be a fool to leave."

"I'd be a bigger fool to lose you," he said simply.

She thought her heart would burst when she realized he was willing to give up so much for her. Tears misted her vision, and a lifetime of stubborn pride seemed to melt. "You really do love me."

He nodded slowly.

"Oh, Spencer. I love you too. I was going to ask you to tear up my resignation letter. You were right. I have to stop running away. I've decided I can handle it. I'm going to be your colleague all day and your lover all night."

"No."

"No?" The bright vision of the future faded before her eyes.

"You'll love me all night, but as my wife." And pulling her forward, he found her mouth with his, in a kiss that was both tender and demanding.

The tears spilled over. "I don't think I'm very good at being married."

"So your first marriage was a mistake." Although there was laughter in his eyes, there was a serious light in them as well. "You might find it's easier with a real husband."

Happiness swelled within her as she looked at him. "Spoken like a true egotist. Think of the things I'll have to do when I'm married to you."

"I am thinking," he replied, his voice muffled as his lips traveled down her throat, hot and eager.

Trying to keep her focus wasn't easy as shivers of delight chased each other across her flesh. "I'll have to keep an eye on your clothes, for one. They're a mess."

She gasped as he nipped her shoulder just where it joined her neck.

"Color-code them, buy closet organizers, throw them all away and I'll buy new ones if you like."

"Then there's all the shop talk. You'll probably want to talk about computers all the time."

"Day and night," he agreed softly, although she had the feeling his thoughts were elsewhere. This was confirmed when he asked her to raise her arms. Not wanting to lose her train of thought, she complied.

"And another thing. You probably expect a wife to cook for you." She paused while he pulled the T-shirt over her head. "I have to be honest, I've never been much of a— Oh! I just can't think when you put your hands on my...oh..."

"I love cooking. I'm a very modern man," he assured her as he pulled her bra off.

Her objections started to melt along with the rest of her as she felt his hungry lips at her breast. "I'm not taking your name," she gasped, clutching at his unruly dark hair.

"You have a beautiful name. Keep it," he said, and went back to what he was doing, sucking one berry-bright nipple into his mouth.

"I'm also not having one of those marriages where household chores are distributed according to sex."

His tongue trailed a lazy path down her belly. "Sex?"

"I mean gender." She cried desperately.

"Okay. You can take the garbage out every week and change the oil in the car. These are very pretty panties."

"Thank you. I...and that's another thing, we each wash our own."

"Panties?" He ran his tongue down the front of the pink silk. "I don't mind washing your panties."

"Oh..." She was having serious trouble keeping track of her objections to marrying him. He was easing her panties down her legs. She put her hands on his shoulders while he raised her left foot, then the right, to ease her underwear off.

"I think you're approaching this from the wrong angle," Spencer informed her. "Think of all the things I can do for you."

His long fingers stroked her feet in a totally erotic way, giving her a few ideas about what he could do for her, but she challenged him anyway. "Like what?"

"When's the last time you had your toenails painted? I'm very good at that."

A giggle rippled through her. "Toenail-painting. That's a benefit of marriage?"

"Don't sell me short. It's not just the toenail-painting, it's the foot massage that's the true benefit here. Although you will have terrific-looking toenails at the end of it, too."

"Foot massage..."

"Well, I could be persuaded to increase the scope of the massage." His hands traveled slowly up her legs while he was speaking. "I don't think a full body massage would be out of the question, on a regular basis."

"This is sounding better all the time. Maybe you should give me a demonstration before I make my final decision. And I should warn you, I like my masseurs to be naked."

In seconds, his clothes joined hers on the living-room floor. She could see she was going to have to train him to take better care of his clothing. Soon, very soon, she would start...but not quite yet. She forgot all about the mess as he proceeded to give her a full body massage unlike any massage she'd ever had before.

Much later, she lay in his arms feeling sated and complete. The carpet was a little abrasive under her naked skin, but she felt too lazy to suggest a move to the bedroom.

Idly she traced lines with her fingertip along the stubble on his jaw. Under her ear his heart thudded strongly, and she listened to it slow, smiling to think that she'd made it pound.

"And I'm going to get those on a regular basis?" She couldn't resist teasing him.

"Mmm-hmm. I can be on call twenty-four hours a day now that I won't have so much responsibility at work." He spoke idly, but some instinct warned her that he was serious.

She raised her head and propped up on her elbow to look down into his face and check for teasing. "You aren't really thinking about giving up your job?"

"I already did it."

"You're serious!" She gasped.

"My meeting with Ed Pospett couldn't have been better timed."

"But what did you tell him?"

"I told him I was going to marry you, and I couldn't have my wife reporting to me."

"But...but you're the President of Datatracker."

"Not any more. Now I'm Vice President, New Product Development." He must have read the concern on her face, for he added, "It's what I love to do. I miss creating new products more than I'll ever miss administration."

"You'll give up your job for me?"

"Yep. And I'm hoping you'll keep yours for me."

"Oh, Spencer. I'm so happy."

"Just a minute." He glanced around the clothing sprawled all over the floor until he spotted his jacket and dragged it forward. She smiled as he began madly patting pockets again, and withdrew a small jeweler's box. As he snapped it open, she saw a simple and elegant engagement ring. "Marry me?"

"Yes," she whispered.

As he slipped the ring on the fourth finger of her left hand, Jane realized that *this* ring was the perfect fit.

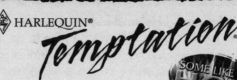

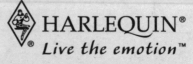

Your opinion is important to us! Please take a few moments to share your thoughts with us about your experiences with Harlequin and Silhouette books. Your comments will be very useful in ensuring that we deliver books you love to read. *Please take a few minutes to complete the questionnaire, then send it to us at the address below.*

Send your completed questionnaires to:
Harlequin/Silhouette Reader Survey, P.O. Box 9046, Buffalo, NY 14269-9046

1. As you may know, there are many different lines under the Harlequin and Silhouette brands. Each of the lines is listed below. Please check the box that most represents your reading habit for each line.

Line	Currently read this line	Do not read this line	Not sure if I read this line
Harlequin American Romance	❏	❏	❏
Harlequin Duets	❏	❏	❏
Harlequin Romance	❏	❏	❏
Harlequin Historicals	❏	❏	❏
Harlequin Superromance	❏	❏	❏
Harlequin Intrigue	❏	❏	❏
Harlequin Presents	❏	❏	❏
Harlequin Temptation	❏	❏	❏
Harlequin Blaze	❏	❏	❏
Silhouette Special Edition	❏	❏	❏
Silhouette Romance	❏	❏	❏
Silhouette Intimate Moments	❏	❏	❏
Silhouette Desire	❏	❏	❏

2. Which of the following best describes why you bought *this book?* One answer only, please.

the picture on the cover	❏	the title	❏
the author	❏	the line is one I read often	❏
part of a miniseries	❏	saw an ad in another book	❏
saw an ad in a magazine/newsletter	❏	a friend told me about it	❏
I borrowed/was given this book	❏	other: _____	❏

3. Where did you buy *this book?* One answer only, please.

at Barnes & Noble	❏	at a grocery store	❏
at Waldenbooks	❏	at a drugstore	❏
at Borders	❏	on eHarlequin.com Web site	❏
at another bookstore	❏	from another Web site	❏
at Wal-Mart	❏	Harlequin/Silhouette Reader	❏
at Target	❏	Service/through the mail	
at Kmart	❏	used books from anywhere	❏
at another department store or mass merchandiser	❏	I borrowed/was given this book	❏

4. On average, how many Harlequin and Silhouette books do you buy at one time?

I buy _____ books at one time	❏
I rarely buy a book	❏

MRQ403HT-1A

5. How many times per month do you shop for any *Harlequin and/or Silhouette* books?
One answer only, please.

1 or more times a week	❑	a few times per year	❑
1 to 3 times per month	❑	less often than once a year	❑
1 to 2 times every 3 months	❑	never	❑

6. When you think of your ideal heroine, which *one* statement describes her the best?
One answer only, please.

She's a woman who is strong-willed	❑	She's a desirable woman	❑
She's a woman who is needed by others	❑	She's a powerful woman	❑
She's a woman who is taken care of	❑	She's a passionate woman	❑
She's an adventurous woman	❑	She's a sensitive woman	❑

7. The following statements describe types or genres of books that you may be
interested in reading. Pick *up to 2 types* of books that you are most interested in.

I like to read about truly romantic relationships	❑
I like to read stories that are sexy romances	❑
I like to read romantic comedies	❑
I like to read a romantic mystery/suspense	❑
I like to read about romantic adventures	❑
I like to read romance stories that involve family	❑
I like to read about a romance in times or places that I have never seen	❑
Other: _____	❑

*The following questions help us to group your answers with those readers who are
similar to you. Your answers will remain confidential.*

8. Please record your year of birth below.
19 _____

9. What is your marital status?

single ❑   married ❑   common-law ❑   widowed ❑
divorced/separated ❑

10. Do you have children 18 years of age or younger currently living at home?
yes ❑   no ❑

11. Which of the following best describes your employment status?
employed full-time or part-time ❑   homemaker ❑   student ❑
retired ❑   unemployed ❑

12. Do you have access to the Internet from either home or work?
yes ❑   no ❑

13. Have you ever visited eHarlequin.com?
yes ❑   no ❑

14. What state do you live in?

_____

15. Are you a member of Harlequin/Silhouette Reader Service?
yes ❑   Account # _____   no ❑   MRQ403HT-1B

If you enjoyed what you just read,
then we've got an offer you can't resist!

Take 2 bestselling
love stories FREE!

Plus get a FREE surprise gift!

COMING NEXT MONTH